BROADCAST

BROADCAST

LIAM BROWN

BANTAM
SYDNEY AUCKLAND TORONTO NEW YORK LONDON

A Bantam book
Published by Penguin Random House Australia Pty Ltd
Level 3, 100 Pacific Highway, North Sydney NSW 2060
www.penguin.com.au

 Penguin
Random House
Australia

First published in the United Kingdom by Legend Press Ltd in 2017
First published in Australia by Bantam in 2017

Addresses for the Penguin Random House group of companies can be found at global.penguinrandomhouse.com/offices.

Cataloguing-in-Publication entry is available from the
National Library of Australia http://catalogue.nla.gov.au/

ISBN 978 0 14378 806 5

Cover design by Simon Levy
Typeset in Times by Midland Typesetters, Australia,
based on design by Legend Press Ltd
Printed in Australia by Griffin Press, an accredited ISO AS/NZS 14001:2004 Environmental Management System printer

Penguin Random House Australia uses papers that are natural, renewable and recyclable products and made from wood grown in sustainable forests. The logging and manufacturing processes are expected to conform to the environmental regulations of the country of origin.

This book is for Elliot and Felix.
Turn off! Tune out! Drop in!

PART ONE

From below, the entire structure appears to be made of glass.

Ceiling, walls, floor.

A giant bubble suspended a few hundred feet above the courtyard, supported by a complicated arrangement of stainless steel beams and high-tensile wires.

A teardrop caught in a spider's web.

Back on the ground, a young man and a slightly older woman crane their necks, open-mouthed. Though not yet ten, their morning so far has been a blur of over-caffeinated drudgery as they attempted to gouge their way through London's relentlessly congested arteries; a Jubilee Line jumper combining with an Uber strike to create a perfect commuting storm. Even when they'd finally reached their destination, their ordeal was not over, a private militia of security guards insisting on all manner of invasive checks and scans and searches before they'd let them pass. Bags. Shoes. Laptops. Everything had to be rifled through by hand and fed through X-ray machines and metal detectors before they were reluctantly granted access to the inner sanctum of the courtyard. The whole thing was a nightmare.

But all that is forgotten now.

Though they have heard rumours about the company's new British headquarters, nothing has prepared them for the impossible scale or sheer architectural beauty of the glistening glass orb that dangles high above them in mid-air.

At least, the woman finds it beautiful. The man is not so sure. He is slightly hungover, and for some reason the building makes him feel a little nauseous. Squinting up, he is able to make out the dark undersides of various bits of office equipment. Desks and chairs and printers and water coolers. The utilitarian necessities of any business, no matter how high-tech. Alongside these objects are smaller, lighter shapes, occasionally shifting from one side of the bubble to the other, fluttering like moths trapped under a lampshade. Instinctively he finds himself sliding out his phone and holding it at arm's length, expertly framing his face and the bubble behind him. He gurns, takes a picture and captions it, his smile fading the moment he hits Send.

'So have you got any idea how long this is going to take? I'm supposed to be going to the gym later...'

The woman sighs. Counts backwards from five. 'Let's just play it by ear, shall we? It's taken months to put this together. The last thing I want to do is appear eager to dash off. You should relax, David. Try to enjoy yourself. This is a great opportunity. There are plenty of people who would kill to be here.'

'Yeah, I know. It's just that... Well, formal interviews aren't really my thing. If he's launching a new product, I don't know why he doesn't just throw a press conference like anyone else. Why do we have to traipse halfway across the city just to shoot a stupid video?'

'Because he's *not* just anyone else. He's Xan Brinkley. If he wants to do an interview on the moon, you better believe the rest of us will fight each other for a spot in the rocket. That's how this works. He's a big deal. He calls the shots.'

She takes another deep breath. Softens slightly.

'Look, you're overthinking this. We need to focus on the positives. Yes, he could have called a press conference. But instead he chose to talk exclusively to you. Doesn't that tell you something?'

David shrugs.

'Well, for one thing, it shows he's obviously a big fan of your show.'

'Yeah, right.'

'Are you kidding? Of course he's a fan. And why wouldn't he be? You're a star, David. You're digital dynamite.'

A smirk, a raised eyebrow.

'What? A million subscribers? Six hundred thousand followers? If that's not the definition of a star, then I don't know what is. Okay, so things might have slowed a smidgeon lately, but that's the nature of the beast. You've been doing this for what? Three years now? You're a veteran. A pioneer. Who wouldn't want a piece of that?'

Despite himself, he feels a faint smile tugging at the corners of his lips. A sliver of ice amongst the spray tan and designer stubble. 'Yeah, well. Maybe you're right.'

'I *know* I'm right. Anyway, even if I'm not, the money that's on the table here is, to put it bluntly, insane. So, stop fixating on the format and let's get in there and...'

Before she can finish, there is a flicker of movement across the courtyard, followed by the knuckle-crack click of high heels across black granite slabs.

A tall, dark-haired woman stalks into view, a tablet computer pressed tightly to her cosmetically enhanced chest. She smiles, extends her hand, professionally frosty. Around her wrist is a slim tracker band, the screen of which pulses with a soft green light. 'I'm Katya. We spoke yesterday?'

Sarah shakes her hand, returns the smile. 'It's so lovely to finally meet you in person. And this is David.'

'David. I can't tell you how delighted Xan is that you could make it today. He's a huge fan of the show. We all are.'

There is a trace of a foreign accent, though too faint to pin to anywhere specific. Scandinavian, David thinks. Or Eastern European, perhaps.

'Thank you,' he says automatically. 'That's sweet of you to say.'

There's a slightly awkward pause, while Katya looks him up and down, assessing him as if he were an item of clothing, a piece of furniture. 'You're taller in real life,' she says eventually.

'Oh, well,' he stammers. 'Well, thank you, again. I guess.'

She nods. 'More handsome, too. Now, if you'll come this way please.'

Sarah and David exchange a quick glance before following Katya, who is already halfway across the courtyard by the time they catch her up.

'You made it through security okay?' she asks as they reach her.

Sarah grimaces, tugging at the plastic ID badge dangling from the lanyard around her neck. 'Let's just say I'm glad I wore clean underwear.'

Katya blinks, missing the joke. 'I'm sure you can appreciate that Xan takes his privacy extremely seriously.'

'Sure. To be honest I was surprised he was able to be here in person. Especially with everything that's going on at the moment overseas.'

'Nonsense. He flew in last night especially. He didn't want to miss out on the chance to meet you both. Like I said, we're all incredibly excited you could make it.'

The trio comes to a pause beside a black marble pillar. Stooping slightly, Katya leans her face into a concealed panel and pauses. Keeping her head perfectly still, she pokes out the tip of her tongue, a pink point emerging from between the crimson pillows of her lips.

On the panel beside her, a small red light blinks twice and turns green. The door peels silently back, revealing a mirrored elevator.

'Tongue scanner,' she says in answer to their bewildered stares. 'Just as unique as a retina or a finger print, and far harder to forge. They'll be industry standard within twelve months.' She pauses, allowing herself a small smile. 'Although you do feel a tad silly sometimes.'

As the elevator glides silently upwards, David takes the opportunity to take in their guide properly for the first time. She's a little older than him, he guesses, though it's not easy to tell by how much. Late twenties. Thirty at a push. She's beautiful too, though in a slightly unnerving way, tall and angular, with a jolt of black hair and a complexion so preternaturally clear that she somehow doesn't look quite real. It's her eyes, though, that are the most startling thing about her. Huge and unblinking. The colour of polished slate. They give nothing away.

A moment later the elevator comes to a stop and the doors split apart. As they step out, both David and Sarah give a small, involuntary gasp. The floor is a single, seamless piece of glass, allowing them to look directly onto the courtyard below. It's as if they are walking on nothing but air. David feels his hangover lurching back into the foreground.

'The team here call it the Goldfish Bowl,' Katya says, taking in their apprehensive expressions. 'Don't worry, you get used to it quickly. My advice to new starters is don't look down.'

Glancing around, it certainly seems true that none of the two dozen or so people working in the vast open-plan office are paying the least bit of attention to their unusual surroundings. Rather, the place seems to crackle with a manic energy. All around them, people are crowded around Perspex standing desks, tapping frantically on laptop keyboards, or speaking animatedly into webcams or headsets, a slew of Mandarin, English and Russian melding together to form a low, indecipherable buzz. Like Katya, everyone is wearing an identical wristband, the screens of which glimmer a uniform green.

'Our marketing and comms team,' Katya says.

No one else in the room looks up, apparently too absorbed in their respective work to acknowledge the visitors.

'They certainly look busy,' Sarah says.

'Oh, we are. In fact, we've just had to recruit again to keep up with press enquiries. Half these guys have been here less than a fortnight. It's a crazy time for everyone at the moment. Not that I'm complaining,' she adds quickly.

Sarah smiles. 'What was it Oscar Wilde said? That the only thing worse than being talked about is not being talked about?'

Katya stares at her blankly. 'I'm not sure I follow?'

'I just mean the negative press certainly doesn't seem to have done you any harm,' Sarah says. 'Although having those protestors outside your New York office last week can't have been much fun? Didn't I read something about some of them breaking in and occupying one of your labs?'

Katya shrugs. 'People will always have strong opinions about anything that challenges the status quo. Besides, Xan is eager to stress that this new project is something completely separate from his other business interests. As far as we're concerned, they're two separate entities altogether.'

'Talking of which, what is this new project exactly? I think you said you were going to send a more detailed proposal through, but I must have missed an email...'

She shoots Sarah a tight smile. 'You know I'd love to get into that, but I think Xan is probably in a better position to answer.'

While the women talk, David drifts over towards the curved wall. By tilting his head a fraction, he is able to make out his reflection in the glass. In preparation for the interview today he has worn a pair of non-prescription glasses, believing they offer him a touch more authority. More class. After all, at twenty-five years old, it's time he was taken more seriously. He slips the glasses off, polishes them on his t-shirt and replaces them. He swallows hard, tasting stale booze and vomit. If he's honest, he doesn't feel very authoritative. He is tired and hungry, his hangover made all the worse by the effort of attending this meeting. There are a thousand other things he would rather be doing right now. Still, this is an important opportunity. At least Sarah seems to think so, and she is rarely wrong about these things. He takes a deep breath. Holds. Exhales. He runs a hand through his hair, mussing it into a loose quiff, then refocuses. He looks through himself.

In the courtyard below he is just about able to see the entrance point where he'd been frisked earlier, a rabble of black-clad security guards still strutting around with crow-like arrogance. Pushing his face closer to the glass, he sees the structure has been engineered in such a way that the various beams and wires that support it are completely invisible from within, giving the impression that the entire bubble is hovering, like an enormous flying saucer. Once again, he finds himself automatically fumbling for his phone, extending his arm above his head in order to capture the view. To his surprise however, he finds the image on the screen registers a nonsensical blur of coloured pixels. Cursing beneath his breath, he brings the device to his face to examine it for cracks.

'Sorry, I meant to tell you,' Katya says, breaking off from her conversation with Sarah. 'Your phone won't work while you're inside the building. Xan insists on installing jammers across all of our sites to deter unauthorised devices.'

Sarah also takes out her phone and checks it, holding up the screen for the others to inspect. 'So it won't work at all?'

'Not up here. I know it's a pain, but it won't do any permanent damage.'

'But this is ridiculous,' David says. 'How are we supposed to film the interview?'

'Everything you need will be provided. In the meantime, I can arrange for a pair of clean phones you can use for the duration of the visit?'

David glances down at the useless black slab in his hand. He feels lost somehow. Adrift in reality.

'It's fine,' he says, swallowing down a surge of anxiety. 'Really.'

Sarah nods in agreement.

'Okay, great. In that case, shall we go and see Xan?'

They allow themselves to be led away from the marketing department, out through a set of Perspex double doors, and along a seemingly endless series of interlinking corridors. Considering the place is almost entirely constructed from transparent materials, the curving architecture makes it surprisingly difficult to see more than a couple of metres in any one direction, and within a few minutes both Sarah and David find themselves utterly without bearings. They follow Katya blindly through a warren of open-plan meeting spaces, all of which are populated by small teams of stylish, wristband-wearing workers, most of whom look to be little older than teenagers. Again, the visitors are resolutely ignored, the young people apparently far too involved in whatever mysterious tasks they're engaged in to offer even a cursory glance in their direction.

At last they come to a pause outside another set of double doors. Unlike the others they've passed, these are frosted, making it impossible to see inside.

'Now before you go in, there's a couple of additional bits of housekeeping I need to get through,' Katya says, holding up her tablet, along with a stylus. 'If I can just get you both to initial these...'

Sarah's eyebrow arches a fraction. 'I thought we signed everything back at reception?'

'These are just an extra set of terms and conditions, along with our standard non-disclosure agreement. Xan insists on it whenever we're sharing prototype tech with anyone outside the company. Of course, you're welcome to take as long as you like to read over it. I can arrange for a couple of coffees if you'd like?'

'No really, that won't be necessary,' David says, taking the tablet and ticking the box marked Agree. 'I'm pretty sure we can spare the solicitors just this once.'

Sarah manages a pursed smile as she accepts the tablet, entering her details in a flurry of precise stabs before handing it back to Katya.

'Fantastic. Well, I think that about wraps everything up. I'm going to leave you guys to it from here.'

'You're not coming in with us?' David asks.

'Sorry, I'd love to, but I've got another appointment at eleven,' she says. 'Don't worry, though. I've got a feeling we'll be seeing a lot more of each other in the near future.'

With that, she retreats towards the door panel, sticking out her tongue until the red light blinks green.

The first thing is the music. Even before the door has zipped shut behind them, they are startled by the shrill jangle of an electric guitar, a series of wild, bluesy riffs piercing the air, oddly anachronistic amid the space age surroundings. The room itself is almost identical to the others they've passed through. Large and sparsely furnished, flooded with a crisp natural light. The only difference are the walls, which are composed of the same lightly frosted glass as the door, reducing the view outside to an ambiguous smudge of shadows and silhouettes.

Nobody can see into or out of this room.

At the far end of the office, a man stands hunched over a small, tweed-covered amplifier, a battered, antique-looking black guitar slung around his neck. As David and Sarah shuffle towards him, he glances up briefly but doesn't acknowledge them. Instead he keeps playing, his fingers working with feverish dexterity as he grinds out an increasingly frenzied melody.

When they are around fifteen feet from him they stop, repelled by the music, which continues to blast out at ear-splitting volume. They shuffle uncomfortably on the spot, exchanging uncertain glances with one another.

Something isn't right.

While the guitarist looks like Xan, he's also different somehow. A little thicker around the waist, perhaps. The circles around his eyes a little darker. Gone is his usual designer suit, replaced instead by an oversized khaki t-shirt, the armpits and chest of which are blotted with a dark dappling of sweat. His black hair is hidden behind a ratty beanie hat, a few greasy curls spilling out around his ears, while his artfully sculpted designer stubble has sprouted into a scrubby beard. He reminds David of a police composite sketch drawn from a witness's memory. Recognisable at a squint, but still a little off. He actually wonders for a moment if there has been some sort of mistake, if the man thrashing the guitar before them might be an imposter, an employee who just happens to look like Xan. But then the guitarist shifts his weight slightly, and the light picks out the scar running vertically down the left side of his face, from his temple to his jaw. He knows then that there is no mistake.

As impossible as it seems, this really is Xan Brinkley.

The famous scar. An ugly thing, like a long pink worm, jarring against Xan's usually flawless appearance. Even now, hidden behind his grungy, homeless-chic hat and beard, it's startling. Impossible not to stare at. Of course, David knows the story behind it. Everyone knows the story of the scar. It's his trademark of sorts, a feature highlighted in every online biopic about Xan ever written. A neat hook for lazy writers to hang the same old pop psychological theories about his famous perfectionism and ferocious drive.

While the exact details of the accident seem to differ from article to article, the salient points are well established. It was Xan's eleventh birthday and he was returning home with his family after spending the day at the zoo. About halfway through the journey, Xan's father was distracted by something – an advert on the radio, a noise from the backseat, the iridescent shimmer of a bird exploding into flight – and he somehow allowed the vehicle to creep across the white central line and into the path of an oncoming HGV. The resulting wreck instantly killed him, his wife and his baby daughter, though miraculously left his son Xan unharmed, save for a deep gash to his face. It was this event, postulate the bio writers, which drove Xan's early obsession with computers and coding, the order and precision of which he seemed to prefer over the sloppy fallibility of human interaction. Raised by a rotating roster of relatives and financially comfortable thanks to a sizeable inheritance, the young Xan initially showed great academic promise, receiving a full scholarship to study computer science at Harvard aged just seventeen. It was here he developed a voracious appetite for both marijuana and MDMA, the latter of which he would later credit for a series of epiphanies that led him to drop out of college after just a single term in pursuit of a more 'spiritually fulfilling' path.

After a few aimless years spent bumming around the beaches and backpacker hostels of South East Asia, Xan returned to the States and moved to San Francisco, where he quickly cemented a reputation for both technical brilliance and an unorthodox outlook. Despite lucrative offers from some of Silicon Valley's biggest players, he eventually decided to strike out on his own, forming his own software company. Initially focusing on online fitness and wellbeing applications, a string of early hits in the first eighteen months made him a millionaire. It is his most recent project though, the increasingly ubiquitous OptimiZer brand, that has brought him to the mainstream's attention, not to mention catapulting him into the elite tier of tech billionaires.

Like most of his early businesses, OptimiZer provides an elegant solution to a complex problem, in this case the thorny issue of worker productivity. Building on the technology behind his fitness monitoring software, Xan created a simple band that tracks an enormous range of data, including pulse rate, temperature, respiration rate, blood pressure, along with a range of other physiological indicators, in order to gauge how effectively an employee is working. The results are displayed as a simple 'traffic light' system. Green indicates a happy and productive worker, amber suggests room for improvement, while red flags up a slacker. It is the very essence of simplicity.

Predictably the bands were an overnight sensation, with factory and warehouse owners proving particularly enthusiastic supporters, before they were eventually adopted by offices around the world. Since then, the OptimiZer band has been refined to the point where it is considered more or less mandatory in most workplaces. Not that the employees seem to mind. In fact, aside from a small but vocal pocket of human rights protestors like those in New York, it is the workers themselves who have proven their loudest proponents. With their sleek, minimalist design, the bands are increasingly seen as a both an iconic fashion statement and a status symbol in their own right, with many people choosing to publish their productivity stats online as a way of promoting their employability. Meanwhile, their ongoing success has seen Xan canonised at just thirty-eight years old as one of the decade's pre-eminent creative entrepreneurs. A raw, visionary talent, liable to change the face of technology at any given moment.

At least that's what the bio writers say.

David isn't so sure. While Xan doesn't exactly look destitute, he certainly doesn't look like one of the world's most successful businessmen. In fact, if he didn't know better, he has the impression he could pass him in the street without recognising him. He is utterly anonymous.

The guitar continues to wail, reaching a crescendo now, Xan's eyes screwed tight as he submits himself to the squall and hum of his solo until at last the music subsides, collapsing into a trailing murmur of feedback.

And then nothing.

A few seconds pass before he opens his eyes. He looks around the room, blinking rapidly as if waking from a coma, before he focuses on the two, vaguely confused people standing opposite him. He grins, his beard splitting in two.

'David! Bro! I'm super stoked you could make it here,' he says, his voice thick with a lazy Californian drawl. 'And this must be your... agent?'

'Manager,' Sarah says, proffering her hand 'Sarah. Sarah Stone.'

'Sarah! Katya told me all about you. Sorry, I'm a bit of a mess here. I was just blowing off steam and I lost track of time.'

'Oh, not at all.'

'Yeah, it's cool,' David adds. 'You sounded great.'

'Hey, thanks dude. That means a lot to me, really. You know I've only been playing for a few weeks now, but I'm hooked. I can't put the damn thing down.'

David shakes his head in disbelief. 'A few weeks?'

'Well, it's a great guitar, which helps a lot. Actually, this one used to belong to Eric Clapton. Or was it Jimi Hendrix? Either way, she's a beauty.'

Xan holds up the guitar so that the light bounces off the battered chrome bridge.

'The Stratocaster. Over sixty years old and still nobody's topped it. It's crazy. They still churn these things out today by the thousand, built almost exactly to old Leo Fender's specs. It's so simple, y'know? Little more than steel and wood and wires. And yet at the same time, it also represents the last link in a chain that stretches all the way back to the Ancient Greeks. Literally thousands of years, each new designer clambering onto the shoulders of the last, until finally they reached this point. The apex of evolution. But hey, don't take my word for it. Have a try yourself.'

Xan holds out the guitar for David to take.

'Oh, but I don't really play.'

'What are you talking about? I saw the video you put up last year. The Ramones thing. You slayed it, dude!'

David's smile strains further. 'Really, I couldn't. I know maybe three chords, if that. That video took an hour to shoot. You should see the blooper reel.'

'Ah, come on. I insist. This is no time for false modesty my friend.'

Beside him, David can sense Sarah tensing. The last thing he wants to do is appear ungrateful. And so with a reluctant nod he takes the guitar and loops the strap around his neck. 'Sure. Why not.'

'Hey, should we be filming this?' Sarah asks. 'It might make a nice segment for the interview.'

Xan ignores her, instead crouching to adjust the amp. There is a crunch of bum notes, as David's fingers fumble for the strings, the mangled first chords of 'Blitzkrieg Bop' ringing out. He winces in embarrassment.

'I warned you I was terrible.'

'Nonsense!' Xan yells over the din. 'You just need to loosen up a bit!'

David continues to strum half-heartedly, his pained expression deepening. Xan on the other hand beams, his eyes shimmering with something approaching rapture.

'There, you see? You're getting it!'

He has barely finished shouting when the music abruptly changes, the atonal whine of a few seconds earlier making way for a sweeter, more polished melody. David glances down in surprise. It's as if his fingers are moving of their own volition, smoothly sliding from note to note. He has abandoned the punky thrash altogether now, spontaneously switching to a series of jazzy chord progressions, his right hand picking out a faster, funkier rhythm.

'I didn't know you were this good?' Sarah shouts. 'Seriously, we should totally be filming this...'

David doesn't answer. He can't. All he can do is stare down at his fingers as they spider their way across the fretboard, his eyes wide with confusion as the music grows ever more complex, a disorientating blur of riffs and runs seemingly plucked from thin air and executed at breakneck speed.

'Yeah, man!' Xan yells above the noise. 'You're slaying it right now! Didn't I tell you it was a great guitar?'

David hardly hears him. He's sweating now, his glasses steamed up. Salty pearls of perspiration slide down his forehead and sting his eyes. He blinks manically, but doesn't stop to wipe them, his whole body gripped by the music, the notes stacking up on top of one another to create discordant yet strangely beautiful harmonies. Sarah watches, transfixed as David hunches over, his hair a smear of brown across his face, his body twitching and contorting in time with every yelp and squeal of the guitar. He looks as if he is exorcising a demon.

At last, just when it seems he will never end, Xan reaches down and fiddles with the amp. Immediately the music gurgles to a stop, leaving David standing there dazed, drained of all energy.

'Jesus, David,' Sarah says. 'You've got to do it again. We'll film it properly this time. Do you realise what this could mean? You could start a separate channel. A blog, a book, play-along lessons. The possibilities are *endless...*'

Very gently, Xan reaches forward and takes the guitar from around his shoulders.

'So did you enjoy that?' he asks, a faint smile burrowing in the nest of his beard.

David doesn't look up. He is staring at his hands, a look of intense confusion etched across his brow. 'The guitar,' he mumbles. 'I don't understand? It felt like… it felt like it was playing me.'

At this, Xan actually laughs. 'That's frickin' astute, dude. I knew I asked you here for a reason. You're right. That's more or less exactly what it was doing.'

Both David and Sarah look sharply at him.

'Okay, hands up. I tricked you. I totally should have told you first. But that would have spoiled the surprise. I wanted you to experience it for yourself.'

'Experience what?' David asks.

'Listen, when I said old Leo's Strat was unsurpassable, I wasn't exactly being straight with you. Everything can be improved. Evolution doesn't just stop. There's always someone waiting in the wings, ready to take the next step. So that's what we did with the guitar. We evolved it.'

'I'm lost.'

'Well, without getting bogged down in the science, we basically re-engineered the guitar so that the strings act as an interface, transmitting signals between the computer – which in this case is concealed in the amplifier – and your brain. By sending tiny electromagnetic cues we are able to manipulate your nervous system, encouraging you to play the right notes.'

David takes off his fake glasses and massages his temples. 'I'm not sure I understand? You're saying you *programmed* me to play like that?'

22

'Mmmm, kind of. Although the buzz word here is *encouraged*. You can still choose to ignore the impulses. But if you relax enough and let the strings guide you... Well, you get to be a total badass!'

'But I didn't feel a thing?'

'Right? And even when you know what's happening, the signals are so small that they're virtually imperceptible. It's totally harmless too, which means literally anyone can plug in and instantly play perfectly, from little kids to old Grandpa Joe down at the nursing home. There's no need for expensive lessons or thousands of hours of boring practice anymore. It democratises the whole thing. Now we can all be as good as Slash or Prince or Jimi without the years of hard work or God-given talent. And it doesn't stop there. We're hoping one day to integrate it with piano, drums, saxophone. It could change everything. If it's ever released that is...'

'If?' David says. 'But this thing's amazing. It'll be the biggest tech story of the century. People will go crazy for it.'

'Absolutely,' Sarah says, nodding in agreement. 'The potential for viral content is huge. Now if we can just get some footage of David playing it again...'

Xan sighs. 'You know I'm pleased you guys are as excited about this thing as me. I really am. But the reality is that there just isn't enough of a market for this kind of product for it to be viable. I mean, when's the last time you saw a kid pick up a guitar? Or any instrument, really? Maybe if we'd come up with this thing in the mid-90s. No, as it stands this is more of what you'd call a pet project of mine. It's just a bit of fun.'

David shakes his head. 'But I don't understand? If you're not going to launch it then why did you invite me here this morning?'

Xan's smile returns. He places the guitar carefully down beside the amp and then wraps an arm around David's shoulder. He leans in, so close that David can smell the stale perspiration seeping from his t-shirt, the sour coffee on his breath.

'Oh, I've got something more exciting to show you than this, David. Something much, much more exciting. And believe me, this thing really *will* rock your world.'

'Explain to me what it is that you do, David. What is your job?'

David and Sarah are slumped on oversized beanbags in a tiny office that lies behind the guitar room. Like the other breakout areas, the room is bright and sparsely furnished, though here all the surfaces – ceiling, walls, floor – are mirrored, rather than transparent or frosted. The effect is mesmerising. While Xan speaks, David finds himself constantly distracted by his own reflection, both disturbed and excited to see himself from so many new angles. Every time he crosses his legs or readjusts his glasses or runs his fingers through his hair, an endless army of clones instantly mimic him. Everywhere he looks he's there. There's no escaping himself.

'Um… I make videos?'

Beside David, Sarah is doing her best to retain an air of professionalism, despite lying almost horizontal.

'I think what David is *trying* to say is that he is one of the top thirty independent content creators currently working online today. As a filmmaker, vlogger, and soon-to-be author, his good looks, fashion sense and relatable, everyman charm have brought him a huge audience, particularly amongst the traditionally difficult to reach 14–17 demographic. Over the last three years alone he has amassed a loyal following of hundreds of thousands of regular viewers, not to mention over…'

Around the room, a billion Xans hold up their hands in unison.

'Thank you, Sarah. I'm aware of the figures. Allow me to rephrase. What I'm trying to get at isn't so much *what* you do, but what the *purpose* is. What is the point of you, David?'

Sarah opens her mouth to answer, then closes it again, stumped. She turns to David, who scratches at his stubble.

'I guess the point… Well… People watch my videos because they care about what I think about… stuff.'

Xan beams. 'Bingo! I mean, that's it in a nutshell, right? You're a commentator. A critic. You live your life and then you talk about it. Simple as that. And people go crazy for it.

They know you. They like you. They value your opinion. Hell, most of them probably consider you more as a friend than an entertainer.'

The assembled Sarahs breathe a sigh of relief. 'Absolutely, absolutely. In fact a recent poll indicated...'

'Of course they do, dude,' Xan continues, cutting her off. 'It's just so intimate, isn't it? No middleman. No artifice. Just you and a camera. An open portal into your life. The ultimate reality show. I mean, forget TV. Video blogging is the *real* successor to Gutenberg's press. You don't need industry connections or years of drama school. Literally anyone can do it. Anyone can be a star. It's almost a shame it'll all be over in a couple of years.'

David frowns. 'Over?'

'Sure. Utterly finished. Within a couple of years, video blogging will be as dead as DVDs. Or the novel. Sure there might be a few enthusiasts who cling on for a while. Retro snobs. Hipsters. The same people who insist on buying vinyl rather than streaming music like everyone else. But in any meaningful way, video blogging is heading for extinction. There's just no future in it.'

In every surface, Sarah and David exchange confused glances.

'I'm sorry, but I don't know what you're talking about,' Sarah says, attempting to rearrange herself on the beanbag. 'David is currently one of the most popular personalities on the Internet. Okay, so there may have been some natural settling of figures over the last six months, but he still drives

26

hundreds of thousands of regular viewers to his channel every week. He has fans on every continent. And it's not just him. I have seven other clients, all of whom are currently drawing a similar sized audience. Online video has never been more popular. Our projections show us making up seventy percent of the total media market share by the end of the decade alone. I just don't know how you can stand there and declare the bubble's about to burst?'

Xan towers above them, smiling. All around them his reflection trails off into infinity. An army. A lynch mob.

'Because,' he says, grinning. 'We're going to kill it. Together.'

Without another word, he takes out his phone and jabs a finger at the screen. The surface of every mirror goes instantly blank, plunging the three of them into near total darkness, the room lit solely by an eerie, pixelated glow. Alarmed, both David and Sarah scramble up from their beanbags. Moments later there's a crackle of light as an image appears behind Xan. It takes David a second to understand what's going on. That rather than glass, the walls, floor and ceiling are actually enormous plasma screens. A six-sided cinema, with them in the centre.

The image is crisp and high definition, and appears to show a life-size hospital room. White walls and pastel green curtains frame a chrome bed, at the head of which is a bulky machine. A long white tube with a hollow circle in the centre, just large enough to squeeze a person through. An MRI scanner.

Xan touches his phone again and the image on the screen changes, zooming in until they are able to see there is someone in the bed. With a jolt, David realises it's Katya, her flawless profile unmistakable, although her dark hair is masked behind a white plastic helmet and headphones.

'What's going on?' David asks. 'Is she okay?'

'Oh, she's perfectly fine,' Xan says, speaking into his phone. 'Aren't you Kat?'

Though no sound comes from the screen, Katya manages to free a hand from beneath the sheets and holds a thumb aloft.

'We haven't got that room wired up yet,' he explains. 'It kept interfering with the scanner. They can hear us, but we can't hear them.'

As David continues to watch, two nurses in full surgical scrubs appear from either side of the screen. In mute silence, one of them begins to attend to Katya, tucking her arm back under the sheets, while the other moves to the scanner and begins to adjust various dials and buttons.

Grinning, Xan turns back to David and Sarah, both of whom are staring at him as if he's lost his mind.

'Remember when I asked you what you did David, and you said you shared your opinions with people?'

David nods, though he continues to be distracted by the screen. Behind Xan, the bed has begun to move, and is slowly feeding Katya headfirst into the open mouth of the machine.

'Well what if I told you there was another way to share your thoughts with the world? No camera. No talking at all in fact.'

'David's already working on his autobiography, if that's what you're getting at?' Sarah asks. 'In fact, it's due out later this year.'

Behind Xan, the nurses retreat from the scanner. Katya's body has been swallowed entirely now, only the rough outline of her feet visible at the bottom of the bed.

'No, I'm not talking about a book,' Xan says. 'Or a website or an app or a social media channel, or any of that stuff. This is a brand-new medium altogether. Something that's never been done before.'

On the screen to his right, an image suddenly appears. A cross-section of a brain, its bulbous symmetry reminiscent of some bizarre, monochromatic vegetable.

'You'll have seen one of these before,' Xan says. 'This is just your garden-variety MRI scan. Or technically an fMRI scan, the "f" standing for functional.'

Sarah nods. 'I had one done on my knee last year.'

'I'm sure you did. They're as common as having a tooth pulled these days. And so you understand the basic principle behind them? We use magnetic fields and radio waves to build up a picture of the body. Which in this case happens to be Katya's brain.'

David turns again to the screen. Flashes of yellow flicker across the vegetable, crackling like a lightning storm over the surface of some distant alien planet. 'What's that?' he asks.

'Areas of increased blood flow. This type of scan is designed to track brain activity. The yellow patches indicate which parts of Katya's brain are working hardest right now.'

David stares at him blankly.

'You've heard of the left-brain/right-brain theory before? Where the left takes care of creative thought while the right is tasked with logic. I mean, that's obviously a wild simplification based on bad nineteenth-century science. Yet, broadly speaking, it's correct to say that each of the seven thousand or so regions of the brain are responsible for various explicit functions. Therefore, by examining which parts of the brain are active, we are able to gain a rough insight into how someone is feeling. For instance, if you look at the cluster of activity around Katya's frontal lobes, you might reasonably infer that she's in a fairly relaxed state right now.'

David looks at the image, unable to make out anything beyond a vague blur of grey and black and yellow. He shrugs. It means nothing to him.

'As I say,' Xan continues. 'This is all ancient technology now. Decades old. Where things do start to get interesting, however, is when we start being able to identify specific thoughts, as opposed to just vague feelings. You see, it turns out that most people's brains are surprisingly similar, neurologically speaking. For example, when I think of a dog and you think of a dog, our brains create a similar pattern. By recognising and decoding that pattern we are able to predict, with a fairly high degree of certainty, what somebody is thinking about, just by monitoring their brain activity. Here, I'll show you.'

At this, Xan once again speaks into his phone.

'Kat honey, could you please think about what you had for breakfast this morning.'

Almost at once, the blank wall to Xan's left quivers into life as a shiny red apple appears on the screen. Though it is perfectly recognisable, the image is not quite photographic. There is a slightly dreamy quality to it, the outlines blurred and shifting, the whole thing shrouded in a swirling grey mist. A mirage made of smoke.

At the sight of the apple, Xan laughs. 'Is that it? So much for the most important meal of the day.'

'But how did you...?' David asks, his face glowing from the light on the screen. 'Is that... What is that? A camera in her brain?'

Xan chuckles. 'Not quite. It turns out that while it's simple enough to recognise *what* somebody's thinking about, it's very difficult to know *how* they're thinking. I'll give you an example. If I were to plug both you and Katya into that machine and tell you to think about a dog, the chances are you'd both think about very different animals. Even if I were more specific, and told you to think about a poodle, the picture you'd see in your minds would still be radically different from each other's. You see, as ever, context is the problem. There's a mistake that most people make about the brain, in that they tend to think of it like a computer. As if our thoughts and memories are like files, just waiting to be clicked on and opened up. But it's not really like that at all. Thoughts don't happen in isolation. They come wrapped in the baggage of a lifetime of personal experiences and history and education and all the rest of it. When you think of a poodle, you might think of your auntie's pet, Fido. But Katya might picture something else entirely.'

David scratches his head, adjust his glasses. He's confused. 'So if it's not showing us what she's thinking, what *is* it showing us?'

'Ah, but this is showing us her thoughts. Or at least, something very close to them. You see dude, we've come up with a neat little workaround. Thanks to social media, people's personal histories aren't such a mystery anymore. Katya here has kindly recorded almost a lifetime of pictures and videos and all the rest of it for us to sift through. Everywhere she's ever been. Everyone she's ever known. At least ninety percent of the meals she's eaten in the last five years. It's all out there for us to reference. So now when we ask her to think of a poodle, we're able to cross-reference every poodle that's ever been in her life and then, in a matter of nanoseconds, and with an unerring degree of accuracy, create a simulation of the one she's thinking about. Super cool, huh? Now why don't we try something a little more complex? How about, oh I don't know. What about your earliest memory? What's the first thing you can remember, Katya?'

Instantly the picture of the apple disintegrates, the mist whipping and dancing across the screen, a flickering snowstorm of ash grey pixels. It reminds David of the static between channels on an old television set, though here there doesn't seem to be a pattern to the chaos. It's as if it has a life of its own.

The three of them keep watching, as gradually a picture begins to emerge, a faint figure in the centre of the screen.

A man?

No…

A woman?

Suddenly the mist clears, and the image pulls sharply into focus. On the screen a young woman stands in the corner of a child's bedroom, sunlight pouring into the room through cotton curtains. The woman looks like Katya, the same age, the same build, although her hair is blonde rather than black. She is sorting through a bag of baby clothes, folding them carefully, arranging them into piles.

David glances briefly at the opposite screen. A storm of yellow flashes across the grey vegetable brain, as section after section simultaneously lights up. Meanwhile, the wall behind Xan still shows the frozen tableau of the fMRI machine, the only sign of movement the occasional twitch of Katya's feet beneath the sheet.

He turns back to the film.

The woman is folding a tiny dress, lost in her own world, when abruptly she turns. Something has caught her attention. She stares out at them from the screen, a quizzical expression on her face, before breaking into an enormous smile. And now they see it is Katya's mouth on this other woman,

Katya's eyes, radiating nothing but pure, unadulterated love. And if they had any doubt before, now they are certain this must be her mother.

That this is her first memory.

She stands facing them, her arms open wide, as if aiming to scoop the three of them up into her bosom. She stoops down, opens her mouth. And then she speaks, Danish words booming out of the speakers that are concealed in the walls of the darkened office.

'Hej, min elskede,' she says.

Hello, my love.

At the sound of her voice, Sarah and David gasp. At that exact moment, the picture bursts apart, Katya's mother and the nursery once again evaporating into a churning particulate mist, before all three screens fade to black. The lights come back on, leaving David and Sarah staring speechlessly at their own reflections, struggling to process what they have just seen.

At last Sarah breaks the silence. 'Incredible. Just incredible.'

Xan grins. 'Hell yes it's incredible! And that's not the half of it. The program we use to interpret the data is getting more accurate all the time. It actually learns as it goes along. With a couple of weeks of solid use, we envisage that the slight distortion you saw there will disappear alto-gether. And with someone like you, who's been filming and documenting their thoughts online for years now, the accuracy is going to be out of this world. Eventually we'll show an endless stream without interruption. Every thought, memory, feeling, even frickin' dreams, all of it streamed in high definition, twenty-four hours a day. I mean, this thing's going to be...'

'The biggest show on the planet,' Sarah says, finishing his sentence.

Both of them turn and face David. He is staring at the mirrored walls, once again trapped by his own reflection. Sensing their eyes on him, he reluctantly looks around.

'I'm sorry, but you've lost me. Where do I come into all of this?'

'Come into it?' Xan says, his arm snaking around David's shoulders. 'You *are* it, bro. Or at least, you could be. Listen. Imagine a show where instead of droning endlessly to the camera about what you thought of a film, or what you ate for breakfast, or what you did at the weekend, we actually get to see it, right then and there. No lag. No delay. No clumsy descriptions. Just a direct feed, straight from your brain to the screen. Everything you're thinking, live and uncut. A constant stream of content, all day and night – even when you're asleep! Forget video blogging, dude. *This* is the next logical step. This is evolution. This is MindCast.'

David glances from Xan to Sarah, her eyes moist with excitement. He watches as she mouths the name silently to herself, seeing how it feels on her lips.

MindCast.

He turns back to Xan. 'You're kidding? You can't actually be serious?'

Xan stares at him, his gaze unflinching. 'Why not? We have the technology to do it. You've just seen a simulation of someone's earliest memory, right there on the screen. This is the chance of a lifetime.'

'Presumably David will be fairly compensated for his participation in this... this experiment?' Sarah asks. 'We've got his image rights to think about. Licensing...'

'Don't worry about that. My people have already started drawing up the contracts. We're working on an assumption of a fixed signing fee, plus an ongoing percentage of revenue. I'm confident you're going to be *very* pleasantly surprised with our offer. You're going to be rich, bro.'

David shakes his head. 'It's not about the money.'

Sarah turns to him, appalled. 'Well what then?'

'It's just...' he gestures helplessly to the mirrored wall behind Xan, to the place where minutes earlier they had watched Katya lying in a hospital bed. 'I mean come on guys. You can't honestly expect me to lie in a brain scanner for half my life?'

Sarah nods. 'That's a good point. I can't see his existing fans being too happy if he's hidden away in a tunnel most of the time? His face is one of his most recognisable assets.'

At this, Xan begins to laugh, quietly at first, then wildly, his head becoming a blur.

'That thing? Dude, that's just a prototype we use so we can demonstrate the tech. No, the actual machine we use is *much* smaller than that. In fact, here. Look.'

He pauses, swipes at his phone and holds it up for them to see. David squints.

On the screen, no bigger than his smallest fingernail, is a tiny, green microchip.

'That thing?'

Xan nods. 'Everything you've just seen, we can do with this chip. The M900. Only one of its kind on the planet. This baby represents six years of research and development. That's actual size, too. It's designed to be worn internally. Just here,' he taps at the back of his head. 'Near where the spinal cord meets the skull.'

'What? You mean I'd have to have *surgery*?'

'There's a minor operation involved, yes. But it's nothing. Perfectly safe. We use a general anaesthetic, so you won't feel a thing. You'll be out the next day. Neat, huh?'

David laughs. This has to be a joke. When he turns to Sarah, however, he sees she isn't smiling.

'There will be a short period of adjustment while the chip learns to interpret the data,' Xan continues. 'But we'll basically be ready to begin streaming from almost the moment it's fitted. The MindCast platform is built and ready to launch. The website and app are already in place. We're good to go. All we're missing is a star.'

David glances down at the phone again. The chip is so small it looks like it would snap under the slightest pressure. It looks like a toy. He tries to picture a scalpel working its way under his skin. He tries to imagine what it would feel like to have something inside him. In his head.

He can't though. None of this seems real. All of it sounds impossible.

'Will there… Will there be a scar?'

'Not at all. We make a small incision just below the hairline at the back of your neck and peel back the scalp. After that it's simply a case of a small craniotomy. Keyhole surgery, basically. All very standard, very safe. In fact we'll do the operation right here, in our designated medical suite. I think you'll find our facilities are a bit of an improvement over anything your NHS has to offer. There might be a bit of swelling for a day or two, but once it's healed you won't see a thing.'

Xan is smiling now. A serene, dope-stoned grin. And yet, at the same time there's a look in his eye that leaves David in no doubt that he is utterly serious.

Behind him he feels Sarah's hand on his back. It's meant to be reassuring. Nevertheless, she seems to be pushing him closer to Xan.

He takes a step forward.

'So, what do you say, dude?' Xan asks. 'Are you ready to be the most famous person on the planet?'

David opens his eyes. He reaches for his phone. He holds it at arm's length. He hits Record. He says: *Good morning, guys*. He hits send. He scrolls through the comments below last night's video. He posts some replies. He answers some messages. He watches a video someone has sent him. He watches a few snippets of pornography. He skims over a couple of news headlines. He flicks through some photos of women he might date. He flicks through some photos of trainers he might buy. He reads some fresh comments below his 'good morning, guys' video. He posts some replies. He holds up his phone and takes a picture of his face. He edits it, using his thumb to smooth out the lines across his forehead, lightening the bags under his eyes, before applying a filter so that it looks like it was taken on an instant camera in the early Seventies. Then he posts it. He writes a comment: *Still in bed, guys.* He writes another comment: *Living the dream.* He watches a video. He takes a photo. He reads a comment. He sends a message. He takes a photo...

Four hours later, David is in a taxi on his way to see his friend Nadeem, a fellow video star who also happens to be one of Sarah's clients. As an ex-chef, Nadeem initially found his niche making recipe videos, though over the last six months he's started performing food related stunts and extreme eating challenges in an effort to attract more viewers. At Sarah's suggestion, David occasionally appears in Nadeem's videos, something she calls 'cross-pollination'. The last time David featured in one of his videos, he ended up eating a desiccated Thai scorpion on camera – a traumatic event that nevertheless turned out to be one of their biggest shows to date. Today however, Nadeem has promised he will not be required to eat anything weird. Rather, they are just getting together to catch up. Although obviously the whole thing will still be filmed.

As the taxi crawls its way through the city, David continuously films himself with his phone. He asks his viewers what they think of his hair and his outfit. He asks his viewers to describe their *craziest taxi journey ever.* He asks the taxi driver if he'd like to be in one of his videos. The taxi driver doesn't understand what he's talking about. He tells David to stop jumping around and put his seatbelt on. David opens the window, enjoying the early spring sunshine on his face. He squints up at the sky. If he tilts his head at the right angle, he is able to block out the chain stores and power lines, so that the only thing in his field of vision is the cloudless blue above. I could be anywhere, he thinks to himself. Barcelona. Barbados. Bali. *It's all the same sky.* It feels profound. He reaches for his phone and points it up. Somehow it looks even bluer on the screen. Even realer. He takes a photo. He crops it, applies a filter. He writes a comment: *It's all the same sky, guys…*

He hits Send.

A little way down the road, he spots a small cabal of teenage girls eating chips at a bus stop, their bulky bags stuffed with school blazers. Occasionally the girls laugh, or chuck a chip to one of the moth-eaten pigeons that congregate around their ankles. Mostly though they ignore each other and stare at their phones.

As the taxi draws nearer, David is vaguely embarrassed to find he is hoping one of them will recognise him. This is something that still happens fairly regularly, though not perhaps quite as regularly as it once did. He still remembers the first time somebody stopped him in the street, back when he was a fresh-faced twenty-two-year-old. At the time he'd only been making videos for a few months, and while he'd quickly found an audience, he was nevertheless fairly sceptical at the prospect of turning his hobby into a full-time career. As a result, he was still working a full-time job, fielding calls for a home insurance company. He was on his lunch break when it happened. A girl no older than seventeen approached him while he was walking to the local deli with a couple of co-workers.

'I just want to tell you how much I like your show,' she said, her eyes on the floor, her cheeks flushing with an awkward smile, her hair a halo in the midday sun. And then she was gone.

Even now, three years later, he can still recall the visceral thrill of that encounter. The disbelief that this complete stranger could possibly know who he was. That she had not only watched but *liked* his show. Up until that point, he'd not even thought of it as a 'show' as such. The videos had only ever really felt like a one-sided conversation. A way to wind down the hours between finishing work and going to sleep. And sure, he'd noticed the views and enjoyed the warm rush as the likes and comments rolled in. But even then, it felt more like a game than something rooted in reality. A way of scoring points. Of getting to the next level. Sitting alone in his bedroom, rambling into his laptop or phone, it had honestly never occurred to him that there were real people sitting out there on the other side of the camera. People who were listening to what he had to say. Who actually *cared* about what he was planning to wear the next day, or who his top three favourite rappers were, or whether he could distinguish between various brands of smoothies in a blind taste test. He certainly never dreamed that he was famous enough to be recognised and approached on the street while he was on his lunch break.

And so when that girl came up to him, it was a revelation. It was like a lightbulb exploding in his mind. Every single one of those numbers on the view counter was a real person. And there were thousands of them. Tens of thousands, even then. And they were all watching him. Listening to him. It was as though he'd discovered a portal into each and every one of their lives, directly from his computer to theirs. It was like magic. And who knew? With that many people watching, it might just be a chance to shed his suit and tie and become the person he always knew he was born to be. Someone different. Someone special.

Someone famous.

As for his colleagues, once the girl had left they looked at him differently. They stared at him like he was some sort of God. All the way to the deli, they peppered him with questions about his videos, asking how he got into it, how much money he was making. One of them actually ended up buying his lunch for him. It was insane. To them, he was a bona fide star.

He went back to the office and handed his resignation in that same day.

By now the taxi has drawn level with the teenage girls. They are still all staring resolutely at their phones, oblivious to anything else around them. David winds the window down all the way and leans out slightly, so he is facing them head on.

Nothing.

He clears his throat, though the noise is lost under the growl of the car's engine.

Still nothing.

Then, finally, one of the girls glances up. She is no more than ten feet away.

Their eyes meet. A spark of something. Maybe? And then...

Nothing.

She looks away. Back to her chips. Her phone. She has no idea who he is.

David rolls up the window. He tells himself it doesn't mean anything. That he shouldn't worry. That this is *definitely* not a sign his star is waning.

That this is not the beginning of the end.

He takes out his phone. He hits Record. He asks his viewers what they think of his new trainers. He asks the viewers to name their top three favourite music videos of all time. He asks the viewers to send him love and hugs.

In the front seat, the taxi driver sighs.

Nadeem is midway through shaving when he answers the door, topless with a towel wrapped around his waist, his upper lip still slathered in a froth of white foam.

'Oh. My. *God*,' he says, pulling David into his apartment and wafting him towards the kitchen. 'I'm so hungover I think I might die. As in literally die.'

'What happened? I thought you were doing that juice detox thing? The Green Sixteen?'

'Oh, I was. And it was going so well, too. It's just that Mike called and asked if I was free to go for one quiet drink and I've only just got back in.'

'You stayed over at Mike's? But what about Chris?'

Nadeem winces. 'Chris was... away? I know, I know! Don't judge me. I can't deal with anything except coffee right now.'

'You're a bad man, Mr Begum.'

'Ugh, I told you, no judging. Just make me coffee, dammit. And make it strong. I need something to mask the taste of shame.'

While Nadeem disappears to finish getting ready, David heads for the kitchen. In most respects, the loft-style apartment is almost identical to his own extortionately priced pad. Open-plan. Minimally furnished. Exposed beams and brickwork. It is both highly stylised and completely impersonal. The only significant difference between the two apartments is the professional kitchen where Nadeem now films the majority of his videos, ever since migrating from his Manchester bedsit eighteen months earlier when his show took off. Like David, it is the videos that pay for Nadeem's apartment. The videos pay for everything.

The coffee machine, like most things in the kitchen, is ridiculously over-engineered; a space-age artefact studded with a dashboard of dials and levers. As David struggles to work out where the water goes in, he spots a proof copy of Nadeem's latest recipe book lying on the stainless steel countertop and feels a pang of jealousy. While Nadeem isn't yet anywhere close to eclipsing his own viewing figures, he has nevertheless begun to, as Sarah puts it, *diversify his offering*. Like most other single interest stars – the crafters, the yoga instructors, the singing coaches – Nadeem's videos seem to exist as a leap pad onto bigger and brighter things. To courses and classes and product tie-ins. In addition to the cookery books, just last month Nadeem brought out a range of branded juicers. There have even been whispers about him opening a restaurant in the near future. Either way, it seems his friend is already well positioned for the inevitable day when the well dries up and the video money stops rolling in.

'Why can I smell failure instead of coffee?'

David looks up to see Nadeem fully dressed, his phone in his hand.

'Are you filming me?'

'Affirmative, Captain. So I take it you never went to barista school, huh?'

Immediately David snaps into his on-screen persona. His voice a little louder. His gestures a little larger.

'Well if you didn't have such a *ridiculous* coffee machine I'd probably be finished by now. What's wrong with good old Nescafé, huh?'

Nadeem stops filming, lowering his phone for a second. 'Fuck!'

'What? What's wrong?'

'I was given that machine for free last week,' Nadeem pouts. 'I'm supposed to be promoting it. I'm, like, their brand ambassador or something.'

'Shit, sorry man. My bad.'

'It's cool. I'll edit it out later. Anyway, how are you? How did the thing go yesterday? The big interview. It was the OptimiZer guy, right? Xan something?'

'Brinkley.'

'That's it. Man those bands are so cool. I really want to get one.'

'What for? It's not like you have a boss.'

'I don't know. They just look awesome. Besides, maybe Sarah could use them to track us? Check we're being productive little video-makers,' he laughs. 'So how was the mysterious Mr Brinkley? Is he as hot in real life as he is on the front of *Time* magazine?'

'He was a bit weird, actually. The whole thing was a bit weird.'

'Weird how? Like endearingly eccentric weird or creepy child killer weird?'

David shrugs. 'Somewhere in between? He invited me and Sarah there to do an interview, but then when we got there it was like he wanted to interview me. He says he wants me to make a show with him.'

Nadeem blinks a couple of times, a strange look briefly crossing his face, before he breaks out into a large smile.

'A show? That's... that's amazing. Congratulations! I didn't know he was making content now? What is it? An advert?'

'No, not really. It was more like... I don't know. Like I said, it was weird.'

'What? That's it? You can't drop that bombshell and then just clam up. I need details. Have you started filming already? You did accept his offer I presume?'

'No. Yes. No... I mean, I don't know yet. Obviously Sarah thinks it's the greatest opportunity ever. It's just... You know what, I've just remembered I'm not actually supposed to be talking about this. I signed a bunch of things which I think mean he can legally have me executed if I so much as mention his name.'

'Wow. Really? You're shutting me out like that? Well excuse me for being interested, Mr Big Time.'

'Don't be like that. You weren't even supposed to know I was meeting him. Anyway, are you going to tell me what we're doing here today? For the love of God please don't tell me I'm going to be eating any invertebrates.'

'Are you kidding? I'm far too hungover for anything that elaborate. I need comfort food. Oh shit, I just need to check, you're not still on your vegan thing are you?'

'Nah, I'm full Paleo now.'

'Okay, perfect.' Nadeem cocks his phone again. 'You ready?'

David nods, fixing his smile.

'So, Doctor D, I've *cooked* up something a little special for us today. It's called the Chicken Nugget Challenge.'

'Chicken nuggets? That doesn't sound too bad. Normally you've got me eating live baby octopuses by now.'

'Yeah, I thought you deserved a break. And everyone likes nuggets, right?'

'I know I do.'

'Great! In that case there's just one thing we need before we get started...'

Nadeem stands up and goes out of the room, still filming. Seconds later he returns, carrying a cage in his free hand. Inside the cage is a live chicken.

'David,' he says. 'I'd like you to meet your lunch.'

Nadeem zooms in so that David's face fills the phone's screen, his jaw hanging open, his eyebrows raised in exaggerated surprise.

'You have got to be kidding me?'

For the next hour or so, David and Nadeem goof around with the chicken. Despite his assertion that *it's as simple*

as wringing its neck, it transpires that Nadeem has never actually slaughtered so much as a mosquito before. As a result, they spend a good portion of their time watching gruesome online instructional videos, clinging to each other and squealing in horror as various Kentucky-fried farmers offer their tips on pithing, plucking and eviscerating poultry. By the time they've finished watching, they are both several shades paler.

When at last they are ready to do the deed, Nadeem hoists the cage onto the kitchen counter. They both stoop to stare in at the bizarre animal. David has never seen a chicken up close before, and he's startled by how *alive* it looks. He wonders if he might go vegan again after all.

'Okay. So when I open the hatch you grab it quickly,' Nadeem says, holding up his phone to capture the moment of release.

The chicken stares back, its eyes as dull and glassy as the lens of the camera.

'Right then. Three, two, one!'

The moment Nadeem slips open the cage door, the chicken immediately springs forwards, slipping past David's waiting hands.

'Damn! What are you doing?'

'I'm trying! I'm trying!'

After a farcical couple of minutes spent chasing the flapping bird, Nadeem at last manages to recapture it, at which point the pair have a predictable change of heart and grant the chicken an indefinite stay of execution.

'We've come too far with this little fella,' Nadeem explains to the viewers.

'Yeah,' David agrees. 'We've bonded now. We're best friends forever.'

The video ends with the two of them collapsing onto Nadeem's sofa with a box of McDonald's nuggets, while the chicken struts obliviously across the coffee table, leaving a trail of feathers and shit behind it.

Within minutes of posting it online, the views are flooding in. The feedback is overwhelmingly positive. Every thumb is up. People are calling it their best collaboration yet. Sarah messages them both simultaneously: *Great work, guys*. She includes a smiley face.

'Oh sweet,' Nadeem says, cracking the cap from his second celebratory beer, his hangover seeming to recede further with every sip. 'Apparently Amanda's having a house party next weekend. You in?'

'Ah man, next weekend? I'm supposed to be visiting my folks. My dad needs a hand in the garden and I said I'd help out.'

'Well check you out, Mr Son-of-the-Year.'

'Hardly. He guilt-tripped me into it. But I have been pretty rubbish lately. I can't remember the last time I visited them.'

'Ah, I'm sure they understand. You are a hot-shot online megastar after all.'

'Funny.'

'What about this evening then? I could invite some people over? We could shoot another video?'

David glances up from his phone. 'Sorry man. I can't do tonight either. I'm taking Alice out for dinner.'

'Wait, what? As in Alice the girl who's working on your autobiography? Is that even legal?'

'What do you mean?'

'Taking your *ghostwriter* on a date. Don't they have a code of ethics or something?'

'Well first off, it's totally not a date. It's just that our meetings are usually so stuffy I thought maybe we could liven it up with some food and some wine...'

'... And some sex.'

'You are so wrong. I assure you our relationship is one hundred percent professional. Besides, even if I was interested, I'm pretty sure she hates me.'

'Why? What's she said?'

'Ah, it's nothing really. Just a vibe I get. I'm probably being paranoid.'

'Probably. I mean, who could possibly hate someone with a face as cute as yours? Anyway, if you ask me you're still hung up on... Wait, don't tell me... Emma?'

'Ella. And no, I'm not. Ella was crazy. Leaving her was the best decision I've ever made.'

'I don't know what to say, man. You just seem to have a thing for psychopaths.'

David laughs, swallowing down his final nugget. 'I think it's the other way around. They have a thing for me.'

As he gets ready to leave, the two friends take one final selfie together at the door, then hug and high-five. When

David retrieves his hand however, he sees that Nadeem has slipped something into his palm. A small plastic bag. Inside are two, lavender-tinged tablets, each one stamped with a crown.

'What are these?'

'They're left over from last night,' Nadeem grins. 'Just in case things go well. You know, with the writer?'

'What happened to ethical boundaries?' he laughs. 'So just to be clear, you think it's okay for me to get high with my autobiographer just as long as I don't sleep with her? Come on, I don't need these.'

David tries to hand over the bag, but Nadeem quickly steps back into his apartment. 'Hang onto them anyway,' he says as the door crunches closed. 'Never say never, right?'

David shakes his head, slipping the bag into his back pocket. He turns away towards the lift. Somewhere in the distance a chicken squawks.

'So let me get this straight. Your mother is an English teacher and your father works in… What was it again? Finance?'

David sighs, takes another swig of lukewarm sake. He is sitting with Alice in a small sushi restaurant, a kaleidoscopic tower of empty bowls stacked before him. They have been there for over two hours, and so far the conversation has been painfully dull, the same inconsequential details chewed over endlessly.

'Uh-huh,' he says, his hand darting out to pluck a passing school of prawn tempuras from the conveyor belt. 'Dad works in finance. Pensions, I think. And, like I told you before, they've been married for a hundred years. They're both incredibly happy, well-adjusted, *boring* people. But I have to be honest, Ali, I don't know why you want to go over all this family stuff again? Surely nobody's going to care about what my dad does for a living, or how many children my older sister has, or where we spent our summer holidays? They just want to know about the videos. By the way, did I tell you about the one I shot with Nadeem this afternoon? It was *totally* crazy. He actually had a live chicken with him.'

As David talks, Alice finds herself zoning out. She sets down her pen, takes off her glasses and screws up her eyes, massaging her temples with the tips of her fingers. It's been a long day. A long month. Of course she's already watched the chicken video. That and another five hundred just like it. She's spent entire nights sitting with a notepad, staring square-eyed at the screen while the man she is professionally obliged to shadow grins and gurns, an endless screed of inane nonsense dribbling from his mouth and bubbling from her tinny laptop speakers.

'That sounds great, David,' she says, slipping her glasses back on and taking a deep breath in an attempt to re-centre herself. 'I'll try and include a section about the chicken in the book. However, what I'm interested in right now is providing some background. I want to show them the *real* you. Not just the guy we see on the screen every day.'

David shrugs. 'I don't know what to say. The person on the screen *is* me. That's the whole point. I live my life, I share it on video. I'm an open book. Hey, do you want to go somewhere else and grab another drink? I'm not sure I can face any more sake.'

At this, Alice's frayed patience unravels entirely. 'Look. I appreciate you're not interested in going over this stuff, but can you please at least attempt to trust me when I tell you that it's important. You have to understand that you're going to be a character in a book. Every character needs context. The reader has to know where they've come from, what they've been through. I'm not saying you have to be likeable. But you do have to be believable. You need substance. Dreams and desires. Hopes and fears. Emotional heft. You have to feel like a real person rather than some two-dimensional cypher – otherwise why would they possibly care what happens to you?'

David stares at her, his mouth puckering as he digests her words. 'Likeable, huh? That's an interesting one. I wonder how many "likes" I've had since we began this stupid conversation?'

'No, I'm sorry. That came out wrong…'

'No, really. It's fine,' David replies, snatching up his phone. 'Oh, will you look at that? My last video has got fifty thousand thumbs up in the last half an hour alone. Not bad. Especially for someone who isn't even a *real person*.'

'Come on, David. I'm just trying to give you some sound advice here. I've been writing stories since I was five years old. And even if no one wants to publish *my* books, my last three biographies have been international bestsellers. Believe it or not, I actually know what I'm talking about. And as much as it kills the frustrated novelist in me, it's all just a formula. Boxes that need ticking. Rags to riches. Triumph over adversity. Laughter through tears. You churn it out and the public lap it up. It's a money factory. But only if you do it right. Which means, you need a strong personality underpinning the whole thing. All I was saying…'

'I know perfectly what you're saying. You think I'm boring. You think that just because I'm lucky enough to come from a happy, functional family and I've had a bit of success it makes me inferior somehow. Or at least makes me less interesting as a "character". Well guess what? I don't care. You might not respect or enjoy what I do, but there are evidently lots of people out there who do. I'm an entertainer. I don't pretend to be high art, or whatever it is you'd rather be writing about. I just do my thing. If people choose to watch it, they can. And if they don't like it, well that's fine too. No one's making them.'

A sticky silence passes while Alice picks absentmindedly at a splatter of wasabi on the table. 'I'm sorry,' she says eventually. 'I wasn't trying to…'

'Don't worry about it,' David says, gathering up his things to leave. 'I don't need you to like me.'

'Come on, that's not fair. I never said I didn't like you.'

'It's fine. We'll pick this up another day. I'll get Sarah to schedule something.'

He stands, throws a couple of creased bank notes onto the table. 'You know, it's funny. Considering it's your job to get inside my head, you don't actually know the slightest thing about me. You might think I'm not very interesting, but just yesterday I got offered a project that's going to change everything. I'm going to be massive, Alice. The whole world's going to be watching me. Then we'll see who's got nothing to say.'

'David, come on. I thought you wanted to get another drink? What project are you talking about? David. David...'

He heads for the door, ignoring her calls. He intends to get a taxi home, yet as he slips his hand into his pocket to retrieve his phone, his fingers brush against something else.

A small plastic bag.

Discreetly, he fishes it out and opens his palm. Two chalky tablets stare up at him. Lavender blue. He hesitates. He has things to do in the morning. Videos to shoot. People he's supposed to meet. He runs his thumbnail along the seal of the bag, opens it. He glances over his shoulder. He half expects Alice to have followed him out. But no, she's still sitting at the table, staring helplessly at her notepad. He empties both pills out into his hand. Tips back his head. The bag flutters to the floor.

The night rushes by like an endless black river, the city lights streaking like spooked fish as David's head vibrates against the window of the taxi. He tries to make out the time but the numbers on his phone don't mean anything. They're just shapes.

It's late. Early. Whatever. He's not ready to sleep yet. Not by a long shot. His shirt is wet, soaked with beer, sweat. He's been out, though he doesn't remember where. A bar? A club? It doesn't matter.

Nothing matters.

He looks back to his phone. He wants to send a message. He wants to talk to someone. He's having trouble unlocking the screen though. The taxi driver asks him a question. He tries to answer but it's difficult to speak. His back teeth don't seem to want to open wide enough to let the words out.

He swallows hard, tries again.

This time the words do come. Lots of words. It's hard to make them stick together in coherent sentences though. Each one seems to spin off in a different direction every time he opens his mouth, spawning new thoughts that need to be explored before he can move on. After a while he gives up. The driver doesn't seem to understand what he's talking about. In fact, he looks a little frightened in the rear view mirror. It doesn't matter.

Nothing matters.

He tries his phone again.

This time the screen unlocks. He starts to type a message but he can't focus. He closes one eye, but it's still no good. Then he has another idea.

He opens the camera.

He holds out his arm.
He hits Record.
He starts talking.

'You've made the right decision. I mean, I would have preferred you'd told me *before* you announced it to the world. But it's fine. I'm just happy you've made up your mind. And Xan is delighted, obviously. I've already spoken to his people. They're sending over the paperwork as we speak. They want to know if you're free this Friday to have the implant fitted? David? David...?'

'I...' David begins, his eyes scrunched tight, his voice no more than a whisper. 'Hang on.'

He lets the phone drop to the floor. Even with his eyes closed, he can tell that something is wrong. Something about the texture of the air. The quality of the too-bright light. This is not his bed. This is not his room. He takes a deep breath, then forces back one raw eyelid. Gradually the world swims into focus. Even then it takes him a few seconds to understand that he is sprawled fully dressed on his living room floor.

'Hello? David, are you there?'

Somewhere nearby Sarah continues to talk, her voice a nasal whine. A wasp trapped in a jar. He turns his head slightly, wincing in pain. A nebula of stars crashes across his vision. Everything hurts.

'David? David?'

His fingers crawl the floorboards until at last he locates his phone.

'I'm going to have to call you back.'

Twenty minutes later, David has made it to his feet and into the shower. He stands there motionless for what seems like hours, molten needles pummelling his wretched body. He is sore and tender all over, his muscles aching as though he'd lunged his way through an aerobics class. He tries to piece together the events of last night. There was the disastrous interview with Alice. Nadeem's pills. And then...

Nothing.

He scratches at a dark stain on the back of his hand. A stamp from a nightclub he doesn't remember going to. On his thigh there is a large, blueberry coloured bruise. Again, he has no idea how it happened. From midnight onwards, everything is gone.

Eventually he manages to drag himself from the scalding sanctuary of the shower and gets dressed. Staggering around his apartment, he finds cryptic mementos from the night before. A full bottle of beer on his countertop. A broken glass in the kitchen. His keys and bankcard lying in the hallway. A phone number scrawled on a scrap of paper in handwriting he doesn't recognise. He begins to make a coffee, but the smell makes him retch. He settles for a glass of water instead, before finally working up the courage to check his phone.

Ever since Sarah's early morning call, he's been delaying this moment. One of the first – if not only – rules of video making is not filming yourself wasted. While makers like him weren't exactly required to provide PG-rated content, a large proportion of their demographic was nevertheless teenage, and on a slow news week it didn't take much for a desperate journalist to twist an off-colour comment into a full-blown moral panic. Even deleting a video was no guarantee of escape – if anything it was more likely to draw unwanted attention, encouraging an inevitable series of suspicious-looking screen grabs to resurface from the bowels of the Internet. Over the years he's watched far too many friends crash out of business after having their unguarded drunken remarks picked up by mainstream news vultures.

Logging in, he sees that three videos have been uploaded, all between four and five am. His stomach lurches. The first two are only a couple of seconds long, bleary interior shots of a club. An abstract smear of neon lights and dry ice, a distorted bass line drowning out whatever insanity he was rambling. The final video, however, is shot inside a taxi. Mercifully it's too dark to make out his sunken cheeks or saucer-like pupils, though his voice is distressingly slurred as he rambles about meeting Xan to his viewers, telling them that he is looking forward to taking part in a new show, that more details will be coming soon. The video ends.

It has thirty thousand likes. He takes a deep breath. There is nothing incriminating here, beyond perhaps a slight breach of confidentiality. The main thing is that it's out there now. It's decided. He's doing the show. Everything else will fall into place, of that he's sure. He resolves to celebrate by going back to bed. There is no way around it. Today is not going to happen.

He has hardly heaved himself to his feet when his doorbell rings. He freezes. As far he can remember he isn't expecting any parcels. And none of his friends would call round without ringing first. He glances at his phone. Already he has received a dozen or so congratulatory messages about the show. Not one of them mentions visiting him in person though.

The bell rings again, shrill and insistent.

Swallowing down a ball of anxiety, he goes to the hall. He takes a deep breath, rearranges his face into something he hopes looks half-human, and peels back the door.

'Oh, hey David. Sorry I'm a few minutes early.' Alice pauses to take in his dishevelled appearance, the look of confusion on his face. 'You did say twelve, right?'

'Um...'

'Shit. You don't remember do you? I knew you were drunk. You left me a voicemail at some ridiculous time this morning. You said you wanted to tell me about this new show you were doing while it was still fresh? And then I saw the video this morning and... Look, don't worry about it. You're obviously still... It's fine. Just a mix up.

We can do this another time if you like? When you're feeling more...'

'No, it's cool,' David says, forcing a smile. 'Now is good. It's very good. And I totally remember calling you last night. Totally. Come in, come in.'

He takes a step back, then changes his mind.

'On second thoughts, maybe we should go and do this outside somewhere? It's such a nice day.' His composure cracks. He grins awkwardly, a child caught telling a lie. 'And also I think I'm probably going to pass out if I don't get some fresh air.'

'Where the hell are you taking me?'

Still too delicate to make any decisions, David trails Alice blindly through the bustling carnage of the midday streets. Though he has lived in Central London for over three years, today the sights, smells and sounds are overpowering. The air is heavy with a rancid fug of exhaust gases and cooking oil, the takeaways that line the road already doing a brisk trade in carcinogen-fried chicken. The incessant growl of traffic sets his teeth on edge. As they weave unsteadily through the crush of pedestrians, he is repulsed by the scum-flecked tide of humanity pressing down on him. Street vendors hawking fake Ray-Bans and Louis Vuitton handbags. Businessmen yammering into their Bluetooth-headsets. Overweight teenagers glued to their iPhones. They all walk too close to him, intent not just on invading, but colonising his personal space, contaminating him with their bad breath and their body odour. It takes all of his inner strength not to curl into a ball and weep.

After a couple of sharp turns, they leave the crowd behind as he follows Alice down a deserted back alley which runs parallel to the main road. Despite his fragile mental state, he is alert to the fact that they seem to be heading into an increasingly unsavoury spot, the dark walls of the passageway daubed with blood-red graffiti, the cobbles glittering with broken glass. As he often does when travelling around the city, he pictures himself as a blue dot drifting across a satellite map. Right now though, the blue dot seems to be perilously close to falling off the edge of the screen.

Before he can voice his concerns, the alley opens unexpectedly to reveal a green wasteland, fringed by a thick knot of trees. The open space makes him nervous.

'Seriously, what are we doing here?'

'What do you mean? You said you wanted some fresh air.'

'Exactly. I didn't say I was a serial rapist-murderer looking for somewhere to dump my latest victim.'

'Come on, it's not that bad. My dad used to take me here all the time when I was little. We used to call it the Secret Park. Although I have to admit, it's looking a little unloved these days.'

'Understatement of the year? This is literally the creepiest place I've ever been.' He nods towards the trees. 'I feel like I'm being watched.'

Alice grins. 'As opposed to every other moment of your life?'

'You know what I mean.'

They keep walking, picking their way through the long grass before eventually coming to a stop before a large, brown lake. They stare out in silence for a moment, a lone swan cutting its way across the water, leaving half a dozen brown ducks bobbing in its wake.

'Look, joking aside, I've been thinking about last night,' she says. 'The meal. Some of what I said was unfair. I didn't mean for you to think...'

'To think you were a complete bitch?'

Alice holds her hands up. 'I deserve that. I mean, there I am getting snippy with you for not answering questions on the minutiae of your life, when you don't know the slightest thing about me. It's hardly surprising you don't feel like opening up to a stranger.'

'It's fine. Forget about it.'

'So you accept my apology?'

'Sure.'

'Okay good, because I have an idea that I think will help us get back on track. How about for every question I ask you, you get to ask me one back? That way, instead of me just grilling you endlessly, it turns it into a two-way process. You get to know me and I get to know you. So what do you say?'

He closes his eyes. He feels hollowed out, his stomach burning, his thoughts slow and tangled. 'You want to do this now? As in, today?'

'Come on David. You know I'm up against it here. We're both contractually obliged to drag this book into existence – we can at least try to make the experience as painless as possible.'

A deep sigh. 'Fine. We can do it now. But I can't promise I won't vomit. So, what do you want to know?'

'Actually, why don't you go first? I still owe you one from last night.'

'I don't know.' He sighs. 'Fine. Tell me about your family. Have you got a family?'

'Yes,' she laughs. 'I have a family. Parents. Both alive. Early sixties. Hate each other's guts but haven't got the imagination to call it a day. They like to brag about my job at parties but openly resent the fact I'm yet to provide them with grandchildren and secretly wonder if I might be a lesbian.'

'And are you a lesbian?'

'Sorry, but that's another question.'

'Damn. Okay, okay. I'll stick to family. What about siblings?'

'Two. I'm a middle child. You know, the forgotten one? Starved of attention, destined to a lifetime of hopping up and down, waving my hands in the air and all that crap. I have an older sister, Rebecca, who is totally fine. She's a teacher. Couple of kids. Drives a four-by-four. Lives with her dentist husband in the leafy suburbs. Just a living stock image titled *Happy Functional Family*. And I am absolutely not judging her for it. Not at all. Oh, and I have a younger brother too.'

'What's he like?'

'Nick? Yeah he's cool. Or at least he was. He's kind of broken at the moment. He's supposed to be getting married this weekend, though who knows if he'll actually make it seeing as he nearly died on his stag do last month. He's currently in hospital recovering from double pneumonia.'

'Jeez. And I thought I liked to party. Sounds like a hell of a night?'

'That's the thing, he didn't even get trashed. Apparently there's some weird company whose job it is to grab drug-addicted teens and drag them out into the wilderness, to scare them clean or whatever. I think it was an American thing originally. Anyway, for whatever reason Nick's asshole *friends* decided it would be hilarious to hire these clowns to do the same thing to my baby brother.'

'What, so they had him professionally kidnapped?'

'Nice, right? Poor Nick was driving to work one day when four guys in balaclavas pulled up alongside him and literally dragged him out of his car. They then proceeded to put a hood over his head, tied him up and put him in the back of a transit van, before driving him a hundred miles, stripping him naked and dumping him in the middle of nowhere.'

'Ah man, that's genius,' David laughs. 'Please tell me they filmed it?'

'Sadly not. Although it seems they did take pity and left him with a skateboard to make his way home on.'

'So what happened?'

'Oh, not much. He spent a day-and-a-half skating in the wrong direction, caught hypothermia, which later turned into pneumonia, and was eventually arrested by some yokel country cop for indecent exposure. As I said, nice friends.'

'Yeah, that's not great. But you have to admit that it's kind of funny?'

'Try telling his fiancée that. He's actually been diagnosed with PTSD from the stress of it all. Anyway, that's enough about me. My turn?'

David gives a resigned nod. 'Shoot.'

'Great.' She reaches into her bag and produces an ancient-looking tape recorder.

'Wait. Who the hell are you? A time-traveller from the nineties?'

'My dictaphone?'

David laughs. 'You know there's about a hundred apps that do that now? Like, where do you even still get tapes for that thing? Actually, can I take a photo of you holding it?' he says, reaching for his phone. 'My followers are going to go batshit when they see it.'

'What? No,' she snaps. 'I don't want you taking my picture. I don't even see what's so amusing. Just because it's not shiny and new and didn't cost thousands of pounds. Besides, it gets the job done. I've used it for years.'

'Okay, relax, *Mum*. But I have to say, you've never sounded so old. I bet you have a landline and everything, right? A dial-up modem?'

'Very funny. Can we get on with this?' She takes a breath, hits Record. 'So, what's the deal with this new show? What was it called again? MindCast? I've tried looking online but I can't find anything about it. And what about Xan Brinkley? How's he involved? I thought he'd be too busy screwing over low-paid workers by convincing them to electronically tag themselves?'

'Now come on, Ali. You know I'm not supposed to be talking about any of this.'

'And yet you were happy enough to talk about it at five o'clock this morning, Besides, I spilled the beans about my pathetically pedestrian family. You've got a debt to settle, mister.'

David stoops down and selects a flattish rock from the ground. He grips it tightly between his thumb and forefinger, before launching it at the lake. It skips, once, twice, three times before sinking beneath the grey slab of water.

'Fine,' he says, turning back to Alice. 'Although there's really not that much to tell. Xan Brinkley – who it turns out is actually a really nice guy – invited me over to discuss his idea for a new reality show. He's developed a small microchip that they insert into me that translates my brainwaves into pictures. Or something. Basically it's kind of like what I do now, but instead of having to film everything, my thoughts appear directly on the screen.'

Alice stares at him, trying to work out whether he's joking or not. 'What do you mean, your thoughts appear on the screen?'

'It's just like a dictaphone, right?' He nods at her recorder. 'But instead of words it records thoughts, along with dreams, memories. Everything.'

'Sounds kind of... farfetched? And you say they *insert* a chip into you? As in surgically?'

'There's a minor operation involved, yes. It's nothing though. Keyhole. No scar. I'll be back out by Saturday.'

'This Saturday? Christ, David. You're really serious about this thing?'

'It's a huge opportunity.'

'I'm sure it is. It's just...' she catches herself. 'No, you're right. Congratulations. I'm just surprised it's happening so quickly. But I'm sure you'll do a great job. Much better that I would, anyway.'

'What do you mean by that?'

'Well it's just I don't always say what I'm thinking. I mean sometimes I think crazy stuff. I'd simply die if anyone could see how neurotic I really am. And as for my dreams... But maybe that's just me?'

He sniffs. 'Some of us are just more open than others I guess.'

'Right.'

They lapse into an uneasy silence. Alice hits pause on her recorder. 'So do you want to ask me another question?'

'You know, if it's okay with you I'd like to leave it there for today? I've just got so much stuff I need to do.'

'Oh. I mean, no worries. Maybe we can pencil something in for next week?'

They make their way back through the abandoned park, neither saying much. As they reach the end of the alleyway they say a stiff goodbye, before Alice surprises David by leaning in for a hug.

'Good luck for Friday,' she says as they break apart. 'I mean it.'

'Luck? Listen, if I can make it through today in one piece, Friday will be a breeze. Trust me.'

David opens his eyes. He reaches for his phone. He holds it at arm's length. He hits Record. He says: *Good morning, guys*. He hits Send. Then he gets up, showers, gets dressed, and orders a taxi.

Today is Friday.

Today is the day.

As he drags his overnight bag down the stairs and into the street, it occurs to him how much has changed since meeting Alice three days earlier. Since then, his life has been swallowed by a landslide of meetings and briefings. Photoshoots have been arranged. PR campaigns have been scheduled. Interviews lined up. His phone has hardly stopped vibrating. There have been two separate medical check-ups where he was weighed and measured. Prodded and sampled. Meanwhile, Sarah calls almost hourly, harrying him to sign various documents and contracts. He is up to his eyeballs in terms and conditions and small print, all of it written in meaningless legalese, his inbox expanding, exploding. He agrees to everything without reading it, scrawling an x in every box with the tip of his stylus.

X

X

X

Buried treasure.

Careless kisses.

Though on one hand he relishes being so busy – busier than he has been in his entire life – he is still slightly uneasy about the veil of secrecy surrounding the project. While he continues to shoot his show as normal, the original video containing his MDMA-fuelled announcement has been taken down, and he is under strict instructions not to mention anything else relating to MindCast until after the official launch. This is uncharted territory for David. For the last three years, he has offered an unrestricted window into his life. No detail has been held back. His numerous one night stands. His concerns about his thinning hairline. His preposterously messy break up with Ella. Nothing has been judged too personal or off-limits. Now though, he finds himself in the position where he is legally required to hold something back from his fans. It feels like a betrayal. Worse still, the lack of information has left a void that some of his less balanced fans have attempted to fill themselves. Already the first green shoots of conspiracy theories are blossoming in the comments sections of his most recent videos. One viewer is claiming that the real David has been abducted and replaced by an identical imposter, while another insists he had proof of a blackmail plot. Though it's easy enough to chalk up the chatter to obsessives and crazies, the situation nevertheless leaves a sour taste in his mouth. He looks forward to next week, when things will finally get back to normal.

The taxi journey is surprisingly quick, and before he knows it he is pulling up outside the familiar grey building that houses the glass orb. As he crawls through security, his stomach gurgles. Bitter metal floods his mouth. Due to the anaesthetic, he has not eaten a thing since last night, and as he submits himself to a second body search he begins to feel light-headed. He had hoped he might skip these theatrics, especially as he was apparently now so integral to the fortunes of the company they were there to protect. The guards remain impassive though, processing him with the poker-faced detachment of a doctor's receptionist handling a stool sample. There is a process to be followed. Boxes to tick. Everything is double-checked before he is begrudgingly allowed to pass.

Although he is slightly early for his appointment, he is pleased to find Katya already waiting for him in the courtyard. She greets him with an affectionate hug, pulling him so close he can taste her expensive perfume.

'David! *So* excited to see you again. How are you?'

'Nice to see you too. I'm good. A little nervous, I guess. But I'm good.'

'That's completely natural. But really, there's nothing to worry about. Xan wanted me to tell you that Doctor Khan, who's performing the operation today, is his own private physician. In other words, you're in good hands.'

'Xan isn't around himself?'

'Ah. Not today. He had to fly back to the States unexpectedly last night.'

'The trouble in New York?'

Katya swats at an invisible fly. 'It's nothing. He should be back by the time you wake up tomorrow. Anyway, forget all that. Are you ready to make history?'

Like the rest of the building, the hospital ward is constructed entirely of glass. Not the opaque, frosted stuff that lines Xan's private office, but completely transparent, without even so much as a curtain to hide behind. After he's said goodbye to Katya, David changes self-consciously into the green robes provided for him, crouching awkwardly behind a heart monitor and IV drip, attempting to shield himself from the eyes of the workers who occasionally pass by. Not that any of them so much as glance at him. As before, the whole place is a breathless hive of activity, the young employees hardly looking up from their phones or tablets as they charge down the corridors that surround the ward.

He has only just finished changing when the double doors gasp open and a sharply groomed middle-aged man walks in, accompanied by a young male nurse.

'David,' he says as he extends his hand, an expensive watch flashing from beneath the sleeve of his crisp white jacket. 'It's a pleasure to meet you. And how are we feeling today?'

Before he has a chance to answer, the nurse is by his side, rolling up a sleeve, fastening an inflatable cuff around his arm.

'We'll administer the anaesthetic here and then wheel you down to surgery,' the doctor continues. 'I just have a few routine questions to ask first.'

While the nurse continues to fuss around David, the doctor runs through a list of things David has already answered before. Allergies. Medications. Medical history. As he checks off the answers on his tablet, David has the sudden impression that none of this is real. The doctor is too handsome, his lines too polished. It is as if they are both actors in a hospital soap opera. They are both just playing their part.

When he's finished, Doctor Khan asks David to hop onto the trolley while the nurse slides a needle into the back of his hand and then tapes a thin plastic cannula into place.

'Great,' the doctor says, exhaling a wave of mint in his direction. 'If you just lie back and make yourself comfortable. That's it. Now, you may feel a slightly warm, tingling sensation in your arm.'

As David sinks into the pillow, he stares up. High above him, he can make out the faint shadows of MindCast employees. Scuttling. Skittering. It makes him think of an ant farm he had as a kid. He gives a sharp intake of breath as the drugs enter his bloodstream, so cold it burns. He pictures liquid metal pumping into his veins.

'Just relax and count backwards from ten.'

David glances down the bed to where the doctor is standing, his face set in a professional rictus.

'Ten.'

The coldness has spread to his chest now, his ribs like the branches of a frozen tree. It's a struggle to breathe, but he's too tired to panic. Too tired to...

'... Nine...'

The world is fading out, his own voice no more than a distant murmur. He looks down the bed again, but the doctor has gone. Unable to move his head or neck, his eyes flicker around the room until he spots the faint shape of a person standing just behind the glass wall at the back of the room.

'... Eight...'

The person leans closer, pushing their face up against the glass so that David can make out a ragged beard. A beanie hat. A pink scar.

'... Seven...'

Xan?

'… Six…'

Xan is mouthing something through the glass. He is trying to tell David something.

'… F…'

Something important.

'… i…'

Something he's forgotten.

'… v…'

And then.

PART TWO

Blink.

I'm awake.

I'm not sure I've even been asleep. All I did was...

Blink.

There's something on my face. Pinching at my jaw. Suffocating me.

Panic.

I reach up, yank it away.

Gasp for air. Then look to see what I'm holding. A plastic oxygen mask, soft and jelly-like. The kind flight attendants use in their safety demonstrations.

In the event of a catastrophic loss of cabin pressure.

My hand hurts. Sharp. Like teeth. A snake? Something snagged. A silver thread trailing from the back of my hand. Perhaps it really is a snake? Or maybe I'm just...

Unravelling.

Blink.
I remember.
The hospital.
The anaesthetic.
Xan?
And then…
Blink.
I'm awake. Really awake this time. I look around. Glass walls, ceiling, floor. A bed with no curtain. A drip. A heart monitor. It's almost identical to the room I was in before. Almost, but not quite. The angles are different. The light artificial. The glass corridors surrounding the room are deserted. I'm alone.

I reach my hand to my head and feel a tight wrap of gauze. A slight sting at the base of my skull. I wonder what time it is? What day? It feels like seconds.

Centuries.

I slip a hand beneath the sheets and fumble for my phone. I'm still wearing nothing but a robe, totally naked below the waist.

No pockets. No phone.

Nothing.

I have no idea where my things are.

My whole head is beginning to hurt now. My eyes feel swollen and itchy in their sockets. I'm thirsty too. And ravenously hungry, though my stomach feels shrivelled and tender, as if I've been repeatedly punched.

I'm about to call out, when I notice a small green light blinking on the ceiling.

A camera.

I'm being watched.

Seconds later there's a sharp hiss as the door slides open and Doctor Khan bounces in. Behind him, the nurse.

'David. Glad to see you're awake. How are you feeling?'

I open my mouth to speak, but no words will come.

I try to sit up.

'Ah-ah. You need your rest.'

Somewhere behind me the nurse fusses with the various monitors. He pushes buttons, turns dials, as if I am a machine being finely tuned.

'I'll brief you properly a little later,' the doctor continues. 'I just wanted to let you know that the operation was a complete success.'

'That's great,' I say, at last managing to wrench a few words from my parched throat. 'Do you think I could get a drink?'

Almost before I've finished speaking, a plastic tumbler appears from somewhere. I drink greedily, cool water sloshing down my chin, while the nurse fiddles with the cannula stabbed into the back of my free hand. When I have finished I glance down, just in time to see the white bulge of his thumb, a syringe of clear liquid pumping into me.

'What the...?'

'Just a light painkiller for your head,' the doctor explains. 'You'll be a little sore for a day or two. This one will also help you get some sleep.'

Even as he speaks I feel my eyelids drooping, my vision smearing to a blur. The doctor says something else, but the words sound distant and distorted. As my head lolls back onto the pillow, I sense both him and the nurse beginning to retreat.

'He-ey,' I slur. 'Wait a minute…'

I lift my head slightly, fighting oblivion.

'What is it?' the doctor says, his voice a distant echo from another galaxy.

'The show,' I say. 'When's it starting?'

Though I can no longer see him, this time I can hear the smile on his face.

'It already has.'

'Well good morning. Or should that be good afternoon?'

A woman.

A woman is speaking to me.

Is that… my mother?

Blink.

I'm awake.

The room blossoms into view.

This time things look a little different. Brighter, airier, daylight streaming in through the walls and windows. Katya is standing over me, her ever-present tablet tucked under one arm. 'Ah good. You're alive. For a moment I thought we'd killed you.'

'No,' I croak. 'Still here. Just about.'

As I speak I'm suddenly aware of how terrible I look and smell. I make an effort to sit up, running a hand through my tangled hair. As I do, I spot the other person standing just behind her. A man I haven't seen before.

'Just as well. Lawsuits can be so time consuming,' she says, handing me a glass of water. She doesn't smile, and it's difficult to tell if she's joking or not. 'Anyway, Doctor Khan tells me you're making an excellent recovery. In fact, you should be fine to go home in a couple of hours.'

I drink gratefully, while at the same time looking over at the strange looking man standing next to her. He's nothing like the painfully sophisticated young people I've seen on my other visits here. His hair is dark and greasy, fashioned in a classic schoolboy bowl cut, with a pair of thick black glasses perched halfway down the bridge of his sharp nose. Meanwhile his gangly frame juts out at awkward angles beneath an ugly grey jumper. Though he's clearly in his early twenties, there's a pale, sickly sheen to his skin that makes me think he'd be more at home in a dim basement than in this glistening spaceship of a building.

'David, this is Paul,' Katya says, following my gaze. 'He's the one who coded the chip. It's him we have to thank for making MindCast possible.'

Paul gives a small nod, then stares intensely at his feet.

'Well in that case, thanks Paul,' I say. 'Talking of MindCast, when do I get to see the show? Didn't I hear the doc say it was already streaming?'

Katya nods. 'He's right. Actually, we went live within thirty minutes of the operation finishing. Xan's decided to use these initial days as a sort of soft launch, so while we're open for business, we're just not shouting about it yet. It gives us a bit of time to work out any bugs.'

'Xan's still not back?'

'Ah, no. Things are just taking longer in New York than he'd anticipated. The good news is that everything seems to be working exactly as it should be. Isn't that right, Paul.'

Paul mutters something indecipherable, still not looking up. By now he's stooping so far forward he seems to be in danger of dislocating his neck, as if attempting to fold inside himself and disappear, an act of human origami.

'We've already picked up around five thousand followers in the last twenty-four hours,' Katya continues. 'And that's with no publicity at all.'

I smile, her enthusiasm infectious. 'So, do I get to see it or what?'

Without another word, she turns the tablet around to face me, pressing her thumb to the scanner. The screen flickers into life. I lean forward, trying to make out what I'm supposed to be looking at. In the top left corner of the screen is a watermark, the familiar 'MC' logo that is plastered around the building, two silver consonants in a loose, spidery handwriting, a font that is no doubt designed to be both kooky and approachable. Apart from that though, there is nothing but a pale, orange dot in the centre of the screen and a view counter in the bottom right, red digits that currently read:

Live: 5071

I stare at the orange dot for a few seconds then look back to Katya.

'I don't get it.'

'I know you don't,' she says grinning. 'That's why you're reading blue.'

'Blue?'

I glance back down at the screen and see that the dot has changed. It is now glowing a bright cornflower blue. 'I thought this thing was supposed to show what I'm thinking?'

'Just keep watching,' Katya says.

I stare at the dot. After a few seconds I realise that rather than a static shape, it is actually moving slightly, its edges constantly expanding and contracting by a few pixels, like a ribcage rising and falling. It's almost as if it's breathing. Leaning closer, I see too that the colour is not fixed, but rather it shimmers mysteriously, from blue to purple to orange and back again. It's pretty, I guess, though I still have no idea what it has to do with me or why I'm being asked to look at it. I'm about to say as much to Katya, when out of nowhere she reaches forwards and grabs hold of my nose, pinching it violently.

'YAGGHHH!' I yell, as much in shock as in pain.

On the tablet, the small dot instantly explodes, expanding to fill the screen with a flash of white, before quickly receding to a tiny red pin prick, no larger than a sniper's sight.

'What the hell? Are you crazy?'

'Did you see it though?' Katya asks, ignoring my protests. 'Pain. We can't track it. Totally overpowers the system — everything's firing at once. It's incredible, no?'

'What are you talking about?' I snap, cupping my nose protectively. 'You can't just go around assaulting people for no reason.'

'But that's the whole point. It wouldn't have worked if I told you what I was about to do. We would have got... what would we have got, Paul?'

'Orange,' Paul mumbles.

'Of course! Orange for anticipation.'

I look back at the tablet, where the little red dot is still simmering in the centre of the screen. 'I'm lost,' I say, fighting the urge to throw a tantrum.

'I know, it's confusing. It took me a while to get my head around it too. Paul, why don't you explain? You're better at the science than me.'

With what seems like an immense effort, Paul lifts his head from the ground, fixing me with a slightly cross-eyed stare. 'So I believe Xan briefed you on the basics?' he begins, his voice a pinched monotone.

'Um?'

A sigh. 'So the electrode implant detects the areas being fed with oxygenated blood and then feeds the results into a pattern classifier to interpret the signal, creating a simulation which we then stream in real-time on the screen.'

I take a long breath. 'Okay, okay. I get all that. But when Katya demonstrated it there were pictures? It was like a movie or something. You could see what was going on. There was more than just this stuff.'

'I believe what you saw was the beta demonstration reel,' he sniffs. 'However, before we reach that stage, the simulation needs to be tailored to the individual. That *stuff*, as you call it, is a precise visual representation of your emotional responses, with different colours ascribed to each mood. It's based on Plutchik's wheel.'

'My emotional responses?'

'So basically it shows a different colour depending on how you're feeling,' Katya chimes in. 'Do you remember mood rings from when you were a kid? It's a bit like that. Only in this case, serenity is lemon chiffon. Loathing is amethyst.'

'So what does red mean?'

Katya laughs. 'Carnelian red?' she says, pointing at the screen. 'I believe that translates as rage. I guess you're still angry about your nose? But I'd say from the dash of terracotta you're also a little intrigued and... Thistle? What's that again?' she turns to Paul. 'Confused?'

'Boredom,' Paul says.

'Okay, wow. So you're witnessing the greatest entertainment innovation since television and you're bored? I'm sure Xan will be thrilled to hear that.'

I shrug, watching as the red dot fizzes with streaks of orange and purple, like scratches on an old film reel. I choose my words carefully. 'I guess I'm just a little concerned that nobody's going to want to watch this? I mean all I'm seeing is a glorified lava lamp. Sure, maybe a couple of stoned computer science students might be interested, but it's hardly primetime, is it?'

'Do you have any idea how many lava lamps have been sold worldwide?' Paul says.

I roll my eyes.

'You're missing the point,' Katya continues. This is just the start. The system has to study you first. It has to learn to speak "David". But once it cracks your code? That's when things get interesting. Believe me.'

'Fine,' I say. 'I believe you.'

'He doesn't believe you,' says Paul.

I glance down at the dot, which is now pulsing a defiant shade of indigo.

'Okay, fine. I don't believe you.'

Katya smiles. 'I promise you we know what we're doing. She leans forwards, so close that her dark hair falls against my cheek. It smells good, like fresh linen, or faraway oceans. 'Now, what I want is for you to go home and rest. You've earned it. Take a few days to recharge your batteries before the tornado hits.'

As she speaks, I find myself staring at her neck, as smooth and pale as porcelain. Her hand reaches out, closing the distance between us, before settling gently on my thigh. For a second I stop breathing. The room disappears.

And then she straightens up.

'I've already spoken to Sarah,' she continues. 'She's on her way to collect you.'

'But what am I supposed to do?'

'Do? You don't need to do anything. Just be yourself. Hang out. Make videos. We'll contact you in the next few days to see how you're getting on.'

As she and Paul turn to leave, I catch a final glimpse of the tablet. The dot on the screen has changed again, this time hovering somewhere between yellow and green, a vaguely sickly hue, the colour of crème de menthe cocktails, or artificial lime.

'Hey,' I call as they reach the door. 'What does that colour mean?'

Katya frowns, tilting it towards Paul.

Without so much as a flare of his nostrils, he turns and fixes me with a cold stare. 'Desire.'

'Ha,' Katya says, a single, percussive note, less like a laugh than an accusation.

As the door gasps shut behind them, I feel my cheeks begin to burn.

Over the next week or so, I do my best to take Katya's advice and pick up where I'd left off before the operation. While initially I'm tired and groggy from the anaesthetic – a bleary fog that turns my limbs to concrete – with the help of a few kale-based smoothies and a strict regime of morning ab-crunches, bicep curls and leg-lifts, I'm back to my old self within a couple of days. I make videos. I take pictures. I hang out online. In fact, if it wasn't for the bandage and slight headache, I could almost forget about MindCast altogether.

After all, that seems to be what everyone else has done, the view counter having stubbornly stalled around five-and-a-half thousand for the last few days. As for my own video followers, they've generally shown more enthusiasm for the oversized baseball cap I've been sporting ever since the operation than in MindCast itself. Or, as one of my beloved below-the-line commentators recently christened it, that 'stupid colour-wheel thing'. Despite her promise that she would be in touch, I've not heard a word from Katya. Nor has Xan called. Whether or not he is still in the US or back in the UK I have no idea. Even Sarah has fallen uncharacteristically quiet lately. Since dropping me off at my apartment, I have spoken to her precisely twice. On both occasions she's sounded decidedly distant, sticking exclusively to discussing financial matters – potential events and endorsements – rather than the show itself. While I suspect my startlingly generous fee has helped prevent her from criticising Xan and the team outright, there is nevertheless a whiff of anti-climax about the whole project, a general sense of bewilderment about what the show is or who it's supposed to be aimed at.

Not that I've been able to ignore MindCast completely. In the mornings especially, I've found myself staring for hours at my phone, something strangely hypnotic about the mysterious glowing ball that throbs silently in the centre of my screen. While the app itself is remarkably uninformative – stubbornly mirroring the stark, minimalist design of the company's headquarters rather than providing, say, any information that might usefully inform the viewer as to what it is they're supposed to be watching – I have used my initiative and located a copy of Plutchik's wheel online to help decode the ball's various hues. Well, I say decode. The truth is that the gaudy kaleidoscope of colours the app spews out largely seems to bear little to no correlation to how I'm actually feeling.

This morning, for example. I was lying in bed not thinking anything in particular, when I happened to glance at my phone and see a particularly putrid shade of mint staring back at me. A quick check of the wheel informed me that I was feeling apprehensive. Now, as far as I was concerned, this couldn't have been further from the truth. I felt fine. Better than fine. Physically I was in great shape. Financially I've never been better. Even without MindCast, my online presence was, if not booming, then certainly steady. Everything was wonderful. Yet according to this stupid app, I was worried about something. Immediately, I began wracking my brain, trying to figure out what it could be. Was it possible there was something weighing on my mind subconsciously?

It was at this point something strange began to happen.

The more I thought about what it was that could be wrong, the brighter the ball glowed, more insistent than ever that I was not just feeling apprehensive, but downright scared. I shook my head, scoffing at the defective technology. Yet as the colour continued to intensify, I began to feel an undeniable sense of anxiety building up inside me, my chest aching with an unfamiliar tightness, my guts churning. Unbelievably, I realised I really *was* feeling apprehensive – not about some deep-seated, half-remembered issue, but because the fucking app was *telling* me I was feeling apprehensive. I was worried about feeling worried.

I took a deep breath, trying to catch hold of myself. It was hopeless though. With each passing second I found myself becoming more and more frantic, my emotions spiralling downwards in synchronisation with the ever-darkening orb of light, which by now showed a chilling shade of avocado – designating outright terror. I was caught in a feedback loop, the app responding to my feelings, which in turn were responding to the app. In the end, all I could do was tear my eyes from the screen, bury my phone under my pillow and run out of the bedroom to make a cup of tea and calm down.

It was a good few hours before I felt confident enough to return to the bedroom and retrieve my phone, by which point the orb was a calming shade of vanilla. I was relieved to see I was feeling relieved.

This freak incident aside however, I have more or less faced up to the reality that Xan's project is at best a mildly diverting curiosity, while at worst it's a multi-million-dollar flop. Even Nadeem, who for the first few days at least managed to feign excitement by repeatedly calling me and grilling me about how the show was going, has fallen quiet recently. Now the only person still showing any enthusiasm for MindCast is, predictably, Alice. In fact, ever since the operation she has bombarded me with texts and emails, eager to arrange the next instalment of our seemingly endless interviews. With the disaster of our sushi date still looming large, and not exactly relishing the prospect of being dragged to another inner-city wasteland, I have invited her to meet me here later this evening – although, judging by the shrill jangle of my doorbell, even that was not soon enough for her.

I've never understood why some people think it's acceptable to be early. As far as I'm concerned, punctuality works both ways. Arriving ahead of time is as rude as being late. More so, in fact, as it normally ensures that the person you're meeting is completely unready, and so already on the back foot. Having spent most of the afternoon working out, I'm still clad in my sweat-stained sportswear when Alice arrives a full forty-five minutes before we are due to meet. With a large sigh, I head down my hall, adopting a fake grin as I peel back the door.

'Sorry, sorry. I know I'm early. I had a meeting that finished ahead of schedule and it didn't seem worth going home first. Don't be mad at me.'

I stretch my smile wider, my cheeks cramping. 'Mad at you? Don't be silly.'

She raises an eyebrow, brandishing her phone in my direction. I catch a flash of coral pink. Annoyance. 'You can't lie to me now, remember?'

'Oh, come on. That thing?' I wave a hand dismissively. 'It's meaningless. Totally inaccurate. Really, I didn't even *notice* you were early until you pointed it out.'

Alice glances down. The orb remains pink.

'Sure. Whatever you say.'

As I step back to invite her in, I see that she is totally overdressed for the occasion, drawing even more attention to my own grimy appearance. Whereas up until now I have only ever seen her in jeans and t-shirt, this evening she is wearing a tight, black dress, paired with matching high heels and handbag. Her hair is loose, rather than scraped back into her customary pony tail, with a pair of diamond studs sparkling through the curly strands of brown. There is even a suggestion of makeup, her green eyes underscored with a light flick of eyeliner. She looks ready for a red carpet event, rather than a casual Thursday night sit down.

In her hand she is clutching a bottle of red wine. 'Peace offering?' she says, handing it to me.

'I told you, it's fine,' I snap, though neither of us need to check the app to recognise the note of irritation in my voice. I decide to change the subject. 'So where did you say you've been tonight? You look… different.'

'Ugh, don't,' she says, folding her arms and hugging her shoulders protectively. 'I was meeting a new client tonight and I thought I should at least make an attempt to appear professional.'

'Oh? I don't remember that being a factor when you met me for the first time?'

'Funny.'

'Joking, obviously. So how did it go? Did you get the gig?'

She pulls a face. 'Who knows? Having met him, I'm not even sure I want the job anymore. The money's good, but the thought of spending months of time in his company isn't exactly appealing. Total creep.'

'Anyone I know?'

'Probably. But either way, I can't say anything. Client confidentiality and all that. Needless to say he's the usual case of all ego and no substance. Anyway, that's my problem for another day. Let's talk about you. So how are things going? The whole MindCast thing is so exciting. You must be swamped at the moment?'

I give a small, non-committal shrug. 'It's early days.'

'Yeah, but still, it's pretty amazing. When you described it before it sounded like some bizarre reality TV show. But so far it's not been like that at all. I don't know, it's more like an art installation or something. Like an expressionist painting. Yet at the same time it's oddly compelling. I mean, I can't stop watching it.'

'Really? You don't find it kind of... boring?'

'Are you kidding? Unrestricted access to your feelings twenty-four hours a day? I already feel like I know you about a thousand times better than I did before. I wish all my clients came with one of these things fitted. It'd certainly make my job easier. But even if I didn't have a vested interest in it, I think I'd still find it fascinating. For instance, have you ever noticed that first thing most mornings you tend to feel apprehensive? Why do you think that might be?'

'Well, as I said, I don't think it's working very well at the moment,' I mumble before seizing my chance. 'Actually, if it's okay with you I'm going to go and change into something marginally less disgusting. Make yourself comfortable here and I'll be back out in a minute or two.'

When I come back through, I'm slightly taken aback to see the lights are off, the room lit by the flicker of candle-light. When I turn the corner, however, I find that it's not candles that are casting shadows on the walls, but the MindCast app, which for some reason is now filling my TV screen.

'I hope you don't mind?' Alice says, handing me a glass of wine. 'I thought we could leave it on in the background while we chat. It's just easier than having to keep glancing at my phone.'

'Er, sure. That's fine.' I take a seat opposite her, positioning myself strategically so that my back is to the screen.

I watch as she proceeds to dip into her handbag to retrieve the familiar dictaphone, notepad and pen, lining them up neatly beside her glass, like a surgeon arranging her scalpels. Content, she looks up, her finger hovering above the Record button. 'Are you ready?' she asks.

As the evening rolls on, I do my best to be helpful. Even though we've covered a fair bit of this ground before – my family, my early career – I find myself attempting to be expansive in response to her questions, rather than simply moaning. As the interrogation goes on, I must admit that I'm slightly disconcerted that she keeps glancing at the screen behind me, as if checking my answers tally with the app before scrawling her notes in that illegible short-hand of hers. Still, after a while I relax into the rhythm of the interview. Perhaps it's down to her persistent enthusiasm for MindCast, or maybe it is simply that she looks so much more approachable than usual, curled up on my sofa in her short party dress. Almost pretty. Either way, with the room bathed in a pale yellow light, I have to admit that I'm actually beginning to enjoy myself.

At some point I reach for my glass and find it empty. When I suggest a second bottle, Alice doesn't protest. Coming back through from the kitchen, I suddenly remember something.

'Hey. What happened to our deal?'

Alice stares at me blankly.

'You know. For every question you ask me, I get to ask one back? All I've done is talk about myself for the last hour. You must owe me about ten by now.'

She laughs, shaking her head as she sets her notebook down on the coffee table. 'Sure. So what do you want to know?'

I shrug. 'Um. I'm not really sure. How about… Okay, what did you get up to last weekend? It was your brother's wedding, right?'

'Wow, I'm impressed. I wasn't sure you were capable of retaining anything that isn't directly related to you.'

'Ouch. That hurts.'

'No it doesn't,' she says, pointing to the TV, where the orb is flushed an indifferent shade of mauve. 'But either way, the wedding. It was… fine.'

'Just fine?'

'Yeah. I mean, I suppose I should be glad my brother even made it after what those idiots put him through. He lost so much weight while he was in hospital. It's just, I'm not sure weddings are really my sort of thing.'

'You never fancied it yourself? The monster dress? The giant cake?'

'Spare me. If by some miracle I did ever meet a guy – or girl – that I wanted to spend my life with, I certainly wouldn't choose to cement our relationship by throwing some cliché-ridden debt-fest.'

'So hold the roses and doves?'

'Hold all of it. If I was going to do it, I'd much rather just elope somewhere quiet, with no fuss. Just the two of us.'

'You and every other wannabe hipster, right? Don't tell me, you'd pull a couple of witnesses off the street, wear a plain black dress and head to some crummy local pub afterwards for sausage rolls and pints of mild.'

'Screw you,' she laughs. 'But yeah. Basically that. Or at least, more like that than the abomination my brother threw.'

'That bad, huh?'

'I'm not sure if bad is the right word. If anything it was *perfect*. I mean there was a bloody colour scheme for guests. Nothing was out of place.'

'It was their special day. They wanted it to look nice. What's so wrong about that?'

'It's just the whole thing just felt so disingenuous. More like a social media campaign than a celebration of their love. They had their own hashtag for Christ's sake.'

'And the problem is?'

'I don't know. Maybe nothing. I guess I just resent pivotal moments in our lives being reduced to nothing more than a photo opportunity. To fucking *content*. Something to like and share and then move on from, everything filtered and framed with the same bland conformity of a fashion spread, an endless popularity contest designed to distract us from the fact that our lives are pretty much totally bereft of any deeper meaning. It's all just so depressing.'

'Bereft of deeper meaning? Jesus, how old are you? Fifty? Because you sound like one of those middle-aged people from the Eighties who used to moan that rap music would be the downfall of an entire generation. So, your brother and his wife spent months planning an event and they decided to use technology to ensure that they can efficiently capture the day for posterity – maybe so they can share it with their children one day – and you somehow manage to equate this with the fall of Western civilisation? What's next on your hit list? Video nasties? Threshing machines?'

'All I was saying was…'

'I know what you were saying. You think you're so superior to everyone else because you still read books, listen to music on vinyl and use a shitty little tape recorder. But you're a hypocrite. I've seen you online. Facebook. Twitter. Instagram. If it's all so terrible and fake, how come you don't just close your accounts? Walk away and live in the real world, ma-an?'

'That's not fair. I'm self-employed. I have to use those platforms so that I can work. But I don't like them. They're too… sticky. Addictive, even. I can lose hours if I'm not careful. It can't be a coincidence that the words "web" and "net" are just another word for a trap.'

'Oh *please*. I've seen your pictures. You don't look particularly trapped to me.'

'But that's the point. None of it's real. It's nothing more than a projection of my professional self. A sanitised, ideal-ised, two-dimensional cartoon. It's got nothing to do with the *real* me. I'm not one of those people who have to share every aspect of their lives with strangers in order to validate their existence.'

'Oh really? And so you're working on a novel because what? You don't need the validation of strangers?'

'That's different.'

'Is it?'

For a moment we stare at each other in silence, the walls blazing molten red. The surface of the sun. The inside of a volcano.

Alice takes a breath. 'Look, I'm sorry if I offended you. I'm not trying to make this a personal attack. It's not about you or MindCast. All I was saying is that I, *personally*, am uncomfortable with turning my life into a public spectacle for the consumption of strangers. I just think it's weird. Some things in life should be private… if that's not a dirty word these days.'

I sniff. The room has cooled towards a pale pink – merely aggrieved rather than apoplectic – but I'm not quite willing to let it go yet. 'So you think we should all go back to the

pre-Internet – no, wait, pre-*photography* – era? Our experiences should be solely for our benefit alone lest we sully
them through the act of capturing and sharing? Get real.
Privacy's a myth anyway. What, you think the government
aren't listening in on every phone call you make? Snooping
on every message you send? I was reading the other day
that there are something like six million CCTV cameras in
the UK alone. Six million! There are no secrets anymore.
All of our lives are public property now, whether we like
it or not. At least I've got the guts to admit it. And more
importantly, the sense to take advantage of it. To *profit* from
it. Take my friend Nadeem for example...'

Suddenly, Alice cuts in. 'David, wait...'

I swat her away. I'm on a roll, and irritated by the interruption. 'No, you wait.'

'I'm serious David.'

This time, something in her voice makes me glance up at
her. Even in the dim light, I can make out how pale she is, her
expression stuck somewhere between horror and amazement.

'The screen,' she croaks, extending a finger towards the
television. 'It changed.'

I spin around, only to see the usual orb, this time throbbing a confused blue. 'What, the colour thing? It always
does that?'

She shakes her head. 'No. The whole thing. It moved.
A picture appeared. A face. When you mentioned Nadeem.'

At the mention of his name, the image on the screen
gives a jolt, the orb fizzing and sputtering, as if electrified.

'There, look. Did you see that?'

I nod, shuffling closer to the screen.

'Try thinking about him again,' she suggests.

I close my eyes and picture Nadeem. Almost immediately I hear Alice gasp, followed by murmurs of excitement. 'It's happening David. It's doing it again.'

I open my eyes. This time there's no mistaking it. The orb has vanished, replaced instead by the same flickering mist of pixels I'd seen when Xan had first demonstrated MindCast to me.

'Don't stop now,' Alice says. 'Keep focusing.'

Without taking my eyes from the television, I picture Nadeem again, tracing the contours of his face in my mind's eye while the storm whips and swirls across the screen. Faster, faster, faster.

And then, just like that, he appears, staring straight back at us, his goofy grin perfectly reimagined. A frozen image. A photograph.

'But this... this is impossible,' Alice says. 'Quick. Think of something else. Think about, I don't know, kittens. Think about kittens.'

Almost the second she says it, Nadeem disappears, replaced instantly by a new image, a huge pair of eyes peeking out from a mass of white fur. As I stare at it, part of me feels like I half remember this cat from somewhere. Maybe one of my friend's pets? Or...'

Before the thought has even formed a picture of my dad swims onto the screen. At least I think it's my dad.

He looks different. His hair thicker, his eyes brighter. Far younger than I can ever remember him being. Cradled in his arms is a large box.

And then I remember.

I can't have been older than six or seven when Dad came home with it. Mum was furious that he hadn't spoken to her first, but I was in love at first sight. What was its name again? Fluffy?

Even as I scramble to remember the details, the image shudders slightly. And then something incredible happens. The picture comes to life. Dad turns towards us. He smiles. Then he stoops down so we can see the tiny kitten curled up inside the box.

Scruffy. My first pet.

As I watch my childhood memory unfold on the screen, I feel a sudden warmth on my arm. Though I hadn't noticed her get up, Alice is now standing behind me, her hand resting gently on my bicep. She is looking at me very seriously.

'Incredible,' she says, her voice so quiet it's almost a whisper. 'It's just incredible.'

I grin. 'I know, right?'

She shakes her head, her expression is impossible to read. Excited? Scared? I realise I have no idea what colour she would read. 'What's the matter?' I ask.

'Nothing,' she says, finally letting go of my arm. 'Listen, I've got to go. I've taken up far too much of your evening as it is.'

'Alice, come on. This is awesome. What's wrong?'

My father has disappeared from the TV screen now, replaced instead by the familiar glowing ball, which is once again emitting a pale blue light.

Confusion. Incomprehension.

'Nothing,' she says. 'Really. It's amazing. All of it. It's a bloody miracle. And it's going to change everything for you.'

She smiles, though it's not really a smile.

'I just hope you're ready.'

'You're trending in Portugal.'

I'm sitting in a plush Mayfair hotel suite opposite a journalist from *The Guardian* when Sarah leans over to whisper in my ear. Today is Thursday, two weeks since the image of Nadeem first fizzed onto my television screen. In that time, events have unfurled at an astonishing pace, global interest in MindCast arriving with the sudden ferocity of a tsunami, comprehensively flattening my former routines and sweeping me out into the hitherto uncharted waters of the mainstream media.

Just as Alice had predicted, within a couple of hours of those first pictures appearing, a steady trickle of coverage began to ripple its way across message boards and blogs and social media channels. Even though MindCast had quickly reverted to its former, colour-splattered abstractions, it seems a handful of devout acolytes were conveniently online to capture the footage of Nadeem, and were soon busy sharing it. Once Alice had left – making me promise I'd meet her again soon for a follow-up interview – I slumped in front of my laptop in disbelief. Already the views were off the chart, my phone propelling itself across the coffee table with the sheer force of the alerts and comments and new followers that rasped constantly from its innards. It was unbelievable.

I followed the action for as long as I could, watching with a growing sense of excitement, until I at last dozed off at around three in the morning. I awoke a few hours later to forty missed calls from Sarah and as many texts again. While I'd been sleeping, it appeared the MindCast PR department had cranked into life, pushing out a series of statements to the media, who it turned out were now *very* interested in the show.

Later that day I conducted my very first television interview.

'Sorry about that,' I say, turning back to the journalist. 'Would you mind repeating the question?'

She smiles. They always smile. I'm a big story. Perhaps the biggest right now. An exclusive comment from me will guarantee her a happy boss.

'I was just trying to get a sense of how accurate, in your opinion, MindCast is?' She holds up her phone. 'I mean, what we see on the screen – is that *really* what you're thinking?'

I nod. Laugh. This question again. 'Well it's complicated.'

That first day after Nadeem had appeared, the app began spitting out images and video with increasing regularity, until it's reached the point where it now pretty much displays an uninterrupted feed around the clock. The footage it shows, however, is not necessarily what I'd imagined when Xan had originally pitched the show to me. Admittedly, some of the pictures are uncannily accurate, almost as if they'd literally been plucked from my brain and pasted up for the world to see. For example, if I consciously try and think about something – my dad, for instance, or a doughnut, or a dachshund puppy – the picture pops up almost instantly, highly detailed and in sharp focus, exactly as I'd imagined it. Other content, however, is far less straightforward. Memories, for example, are often displayed as little more than vague shadows, often out of sequence and filled with yawning gaps of pixelated blackness so that it's impossible to understand what's going on. It's funny – until MindCast I'd always assumed that I was more or less like a walking CCTV camera, recording everything in my path before storing it away on some biological hard drive, ready for me to play back whenever I like. The memories that appear on MindCast are nothing like that though. I've noticed the older they are, the more distorted they tend to be, the picture stuttering like a bad stream, or a pirate DVD. Even when you can grasp the thread of a narrative, the details are often fluid, faces flickering, the colour of clothes or cars constantly changing as I struggle to fill the blanks in events that took place years, or even decades ago.

Other types of thought are even more confusing. Feelings are still categorised by colour, though instead of the dull reliability of the orb, my emotions are now integrated into the feed, colouring the pictures themselves. A sad memory involving my mother might turn her face bright blue, for example, whereas last year's holiday in Tenerife tints the beach a fond shade of ochre, adding yet another layer of surrealism to the feed. This is especially apparent when a memory or thought triggers simultaneous feelings, meaning the corresponding picture on MindCast ends up looking like an image reflected in a puddle of oil. A petrochemical rainbow.

In addition to these psychedelic nightmares, words have recently begun appearing on the screen, rising from the digital mist without warning. Normally these take the form of a single noun or adjective, which may or may not directly relate to whatever is consciously on my mind. So, I might think about my bed and the word 'comfortable' might appear. Equally I might spot a pigeon and for no conceivable reason the word 'refrigerator' might materialise. Sometimes longer sentences turn up too, my internal narrative spelled out in faltering subtitles at the bottom of the screen. I say sentences, though more often than not they don't make any sense. Rather they're just strings of gibberish, as if tapped out by a gin-addled stenographer. This can be particularly amusing when these subtitles are audible. For just as I heard Katya's mother speaking to her across the years, there is also a soundtrack to my thoughts, though one that is strange and often difficult to understand. The nonsense subtitles are pronounced phonetically, delivered with the same deadpan intonation as a sat nav. Garbled snatches of conversations also emerge, the words warped and warbling, as if recorded underwater, competing with misremembered melodies from Top Forty hits and phrases from childhood nursery rhymes and jingles from radio adverts, as well as a whole other host of·indecipherable clangs and chimes and crashes that make up the alphabet soup of my subconscious.

Incidentally, I've noticed most people prefer to leave the app on mute.

Taken together, this bizarre collage of sound and video and images lend MindCast the anarchic, hallucinatory quality of an acid trip. It's quite unlike anything I've seen before. Not that I spend much time sitting in front of it. In fact, I actually find it pretty uncomfortable to watch for any length of time at all. Just as with the coloured orb, I've noticed that seeing my thoughts playing out on the screen has the same annoying habit of drawing to my attention things I wasn't really aware of, again creating a sort of psychic feedback loop. More than once, I've glanced down at the open app to see the outline of something that until that moment had been hovering on the very outer periphery of my consciousness, something I wasn't even really aware was on my mind – an ex-girlfriend, or a lost t-shirt for example – only for it to immediately crystallise in both my head and on the screen. The act of seeing then seems to reaffirm it, to make it solid, until finally the image becomes unstable and begins to shudder and shake and my eye begins to twitch and my temples ache and

I have to stuff my phone into my pocket and walk away to calm down.

Yet as messy and difficult to watch as it is, the show is still undeniably popular. To my amazement, the view counter was registering a million views within a day or two of the first images appearing, and has continued to tick on ever since, now hovering at just below thirty million.

'In what way is it complicated?' the journalist asks. She is excited now. She senses her exclusive. Some tasty morsel she can use to bait her article.

Beside me, Sarah shifts pointedly in her chair. She doesn't say anything. She doesn't need to.

'Sorry, I misspoke,' I shrug, reverting to the official copy I've already regurgitated half a dozen times this morning. 'It's all just so new to me, you know? What I meant to say was that everything you see on the screen is exactly how it appears in my head. It's spookily accurate.'

'Which is what has made the show such a hit with a global audience,' Sarah chimes in. 'In fact I've just heard that Portugal are the latest country in which David has gone viral.'

The journalist sags.

After fielding another two or three well-trodden questions, I bid my interviewer goodbye and Sarah leads me out of the hotel room and down to the lobby. When we get outside, I see a small group of MindCast fans are huddled by the doors along with the paparazzi, a number of them wearing cheap t-shirts emblazoned with my face. When they catch sight of me, a squeal goes up – they are mostly teenagers – and they swarm around me. While Sarah looks perturbed, I make an effort to stand there and talk to them for a few minutes, giving hugs and posing for selfies. While I'm mingling, I notice that every single one of them keeps their phone out, the MindCast app open. They seem torn, their eyes flickering between their screens and me until Sarah finally drags me away, steering me towards the waiting minivan. As I scramble into the back seat, I hear a scream go up from one of the girls. 'Oh my God, did you see that? He was thinking about me. I was right there on the screen...'

Seconds later the door slams shut behind me. The van pulls off and I peer through the tinted glass of the back window, slightly disappointed that none of the girls have chased after me. In truth, they all seem too absorbed in their phones to even notice I've gone.

'We could really do with nailing down where we're at with image rights,' Sarah sniffs. 'We're losing a fortune in merchandising opportunities. Have you heard from Xan lately? I've tried calling his office but his people aren't exactly forthcoming.'

She looks even more tired than usual, her eyes red, her skin deathly pale. I wonder if she's coming down with something. 'Nope,' I shrug. 'I haven't heard a thing.'

It's true. Despite Katya's frequent reassurances that he's loving the show and is planning to catch up with me just as soon as he's back in the UK, I still haven't spoken to Xan since our first meeting last month. It's not only my life he's disappeared from though. He seems to have dropped out of the public eye altogether. Not that you'd notice by scanning the media. MindCast's sudden popularity has brought a surge of interest in Xan. Yet not one of the hundreds of articles that have appeared online over the last few days contain anything new from the man himself. What few quotes there are have been culled from old interviews, the same old story recycled, over and over again. Stranger still is the fact his various social media accounts have fallen quiet lately. Sure, they're still there. Indeed they're still technically active. But reading through his posts, he doesn't seem to have personally written anything for months. Rather, his timeline is simply a series of bland reposted links and shares that look either automated or sent by a member of his team. Unlike Katya's accounts – which I've also found myself returning to, especially late at night – there are no videos, no comments. What few images are there are simply old publicity shots. There's nothing personal or candid or insightful. It's confusing. You'd think he'd want to take advantage of the spotlight, yet it seems the opposite is true. Like a spider scurrying away from a lifted rock, Xan prefers the shadows to the hot glare of publicity.

As the car weaves through the traffic, the city outside appears to fold in on itself, the buildings stacking ever higher, squeezing out the sky. In my jacket pocket, my phone starts to snarl. I slide it out. It's Alice, more than likely trying to schedule another interview. My thumb hovers over the screen for a moment, before I select the red cross. Call rejected.

'That reminds me,' Sarah says. 'How *is* the book going? On schedule?'

I turn to her, momentarily confused before I spot she has MindCast open on her phone, a faint impression of Alice's face still visible on the screen, like a watermark, a ghost.

'It's all good. Alice promises we've got one last interview to do and that should wrap it up. Mind you, she's said that the last three times we've met.'

Sarah doesn't look up. 'Well, see you do what she says. I know you don't attach much importance to this book, but until we get a handle on this licensing thing, a book is as good a product as any. With the numbers you're pulling at the moment, there's potential for huge sales.'

I nod. 'I know, I know. I'll meet her soon. It's just been such a crazy few weeks and... Hey, why are we stopping here?'

Sarah sighs. 'We're doing a one-thirty profile piece with *Grazia* over lunch. Honestly David, this is all in your diary. I sometimes wonder if you even look at the damn thing.'

'Of course I don't. That's what I pay you for.' I grin, unbuckle my seatbelt. 'Besides, you should take it as a compliment. It shows how much I trust you.'

Sarah doesn't answer.

As it happens, I recognise the restaurant from a video review Nadeem posted a few months back. Eddie Lee's is a Cockney-Thai fusion place whose strapline runs 'East Asia meets East End'. My heart sinks. Still, the waitress seems delighted to greet us at the door, casually dropping in that she's a huge fan of MindCast as she leads us to our table, which is positioned in the very middle of the bustling restaurant.

The journalist is already waiting for us and we immediately get down to business, the interview unfolding in much the same manner as the dozen or so others I've done so far this week. The questions aren't exactly probing – I suspect that most of her article is already written, a copy-and-paste job from Wikipedia – and the only vaguely prickly moment comes when she asks whether I feel traditional videos are still a relevant format in the light of MindCast. The question catches me off guard. It's been almost a fortnight since I last uploaded anything of my own, ever since I was asked – or rather ordered – by Katya to stop making videos. Apparently they represent a 'conflict of interest', something which Sarah has since sheepishly admitted to noticing in my contract.

Conflict or not, there is also the more practical security issue to consider. Ever since MindCast started streaming more accurately, anything that requires a password has become instantly off limits. That includes not only my video channel, but my email and social media accounts – all of which are now being managed by Xan's army of public relations executives. I've even had my bank cards taken from me, having been told it's now only safe for me to use cash.

All of these thoughts evidently cause some ripples on the MindCast app, as the *Grazia* lady seems to get very excited for a moment while staring at her phone, before Sarah jumps in with a tedious spiel about consolidating my output and eventually the woman loses interest and lets it go.

The food, when it finally arrives, is more traumatic than I'd feared. I've opted for the innocuous-sounding Knees Up Tom Yum Soup, but when it arrives I find the shrimp has been swapped for rollmops, the grey lumps of herring floating like bloated corpses in a puddle of blood. I don't manage more than a few mouthfuls, though I wave the waitress away when she comes over looking concerned.

'Big breakfast,' I say, smiling as I pat my empty stomach.

At last the interview stutters to a stop. Plates are cleared, desserts are declined. A bill appears. The journalist brandishes an expense card, punches in her PIN. Mints are sucked. Just as we are standing to leave however, a man in gleaming chef's whites thunders towards us, his face redder than my inedible Tom Yum soup.

'Is there a problem here?' he asks, his jaw clenched with the effort of not screaming at me.

I glance at Sarah, bewildered. 'Umm...?'

'I spoke to Suzie,' the chef says, taking a step towards me. 'Your waitress. She told me you said everything was fine.'

'Sorry, I'm still not following?'

'Cut the crap.'

Around us I can sense diners looking over, evidently sensing a drama unfolding. Beside me the *Grazia* lady licks her lips.

'If you had a problem with the food, why not be a man and come and talk to me about it?' he continues. 'Why act like a coward and just sit there thinking all this negative crap about my establishment?'

It's at this moment I notice the mobile phone clenched in the chef's enormous fist. I can't see the screen, but I already know what's on there.

'Listen…' I begin, but he cuts me off.

'No, *you* listen. I've worked incredibly hard to get this business off the ground. I've made sacrifices. Destroyed relationships. I haven't read my kid a bedtime story in two years. I've put my fucking *soul* into this place. And then you turn up and start throwing your vile, hateful *opinions* around…'

'Now hang on. I was perfectly polite to your waitress.'

'That's the whole point. Rather than telling her you didn't like the food, you let the million or so people watching your stupid show know how crummy you thought it was. Have you got any kind of idea the damage that kind of exposure does? Or the lives that will be wrecked if this place goes under? Well, do you?'

'I didn't mean to… I'm sorry.'

'Okay, that's enough,' Sarah says, gripping my shoulder and steering me away.

'You can expect to hear from my lawyer,' the chef yells. 'Oh, and consider yourself banned for life, asshole. Don't ever come back, you hear me?'

As we pick our way between the crowded tables, I glance at the other diners. To my surprise I see they aren't craning their necks to look at us. Rather, every single person there is staring at their phone. Again, I don't need to see the screens to know what they're watching.

Outside the restaurant we say an awkward goodbye to the journalist, apologising profusely, though in truth she seems delighted to have been there to witness the fiasco. After she's gone, Sarah reaches into her bag and produces a cigarette. It strikes me that I've never seen her smoke before.

'Well that was a fucking shit show,' she says, exhaling a lungful of smoke.

I nod dolefully. 'I just can't believe how upset that guy was. I feel terrible. If I'd known he was watching the show I would never have… I mean, I just don't like having jellied eel in my pad thai. Is that such a crime?'

Sarah shrugs. 'Who knows? It could be, in the hands of the right lawyer. I hate to say it, but you're going to have to try and rein yourself in. I mean it, David. Otherwise someone really is going to end up suing for libel.'

'Hang on a minute. So you're saying it's illegal to have an opinion now? But that's my whole thing. Even Xan said so. I'm a commentator. A critic. If I can't express my opinion then… then what's the point of me?'

'All I'm saying is that you need to be more responsible with your thoughts or you're going to find yourself in a whole heap of trouble.'

'But...' I begin to argue, before I catch the look on Sarah's face. She takes a final drag of her cigarette, drops it to the floor, and crushes it precisely under her Louboutin heel. It seems the conversation is over.

'Come on,' she says through a haze of smoke. 'We're late for your two o'clock.'

Days pass. Months.

Welcome to the voicemail of...

I hang up. Nadeem isn't answering his phone. Nadeem hasn't been answering his phone for days. Nadeem isn't talking to me.

This in itself isn't that unusual. Considering we're supposed to be best friends, Nadeem can be both jealous and paranoid. We have a long and rich history of petty squabbles. This time feels different somehow. More permanent. It started a week ago, when he sent me a link to his latest video. Ostensibly he was looking for feedback, although obviously I knew the real reason. Ever since MindCast exploded, people haven't stopped sending me things. Petitions. Show reels. Demos. Everyone's looking for free publicity, for their moment in the sun. I'm just the latest platform, beaming live to an audience of millions. Lately it's got so bad that I've had to get Sarah to start vetting my mail.

Still, I guess that's better than people asking me *not* to think about them. That's happened a surprising number of times too. From film distributors, keen for me not to give away the twist in the movie I've just watched, to my own father. Though I note he didn't have the guts to talk to me himself. Rather, my mum called to explain that, while they're both pleased to see me doing so well, Dad would prefer it if I didn't keep dwelling on my own childhood beatings whenever I see a kid misbehaving in public. I put it to her that if Dad was so embarrassed about people finding out he spanked me as a child, then perhaps he should have thought twice before he did it?

'It's not that, love,' she simpered. 'It's just in our day these things used to be, well...'

'Private?' I finished for her. 'Yeah well, in your day you also only had three television channels and you could buy a house for a hundred quid, so I think we can both agree things have moved on somewhat since then.'

Anyway, I was disappointed when Nadeem asked me to look at his video. My parents are one thing, but this is my best friend. He's not supposed to be so transparent. Besides, it's not like he's ever shown the slightest bit of interest in what I think before.

Still, he nagged me so much that against my better judgement I gave in and clicked his stupid link. And I watched his stupid video. And even though I remembered what happened at the Thai restaurant, and Sarah's advice to hold back, in the end I couldn't help myself.

I thought the video sucked. Or at least, I thought it could be better. Still, I wasn't worried. I was sure Nadeem would value my honest critical input above empty platitudes. Surely, that would be more valuable to him in the long run?

About five minutes after I finished watching the video, my phone started exploding with messages. I was jealous. I was a backstabber. I was trying to sabotage his career. Since then I've heard nothing. He won't answer my calls. He won't return my messages. Three years of friendship. Over. Just like that.

After listening to Nadeem's voicemail another few times I give up and go to find some breakfast. Not that I'm especially hungry. Days and weeks tend to bleed into each other so much lately that I feel obliged to respect arbitrary meal times, if only as a way to ensure some vague semblance of structure in my life. It's as if my twelve o'clock avocado and crayfish wrap is a tent pole, without which everything else would simply collapse. When I get to the kitchen though, there's no food. I've still not really adjusted to being properly famous yet, and so haven't come to terms with the fact I can no longer pop to the supermarket without being crushed by the mob of MindCast fans who swarm around my apartment night and day, clutching their homemade banners and their fake t-shirts and their selfie sticks. It's just insane.

Giving up on searching my cupboards, I instead take a couple of seconds to visualise a hot pepperoni pizza, in as much detail as I can muster. A crisp crust. Molten mozzarella.

A dark circle of grease beginning to show through the thin cardboard delivery box. This is something I've started to do a fair bit over the last few weeks, with a surprising degree of success. Knowing that companies are desperate to promote their brand, I simply imagine something I need or want – a new pair of trainers, a Chinese takeaway – and more often than not it'll arrive at my door within an hour. I used to do something similar when I was working on my videos, accepting freebies in return for review. This is just a scaled-up version. I guess it's the closest thing I have to a superpower.

While I wait for the pizza to appear, I wander around my apartment. The treadmill of interviews has ground to a halt recently, and though I am loath to admit it, I have increasingly found myself at a loose end, struggling to fill my days. It's strange. I always thought that fame – genuine, restaurant-reservation-bumping, crazed-fans-chasing-me-down-the-street fame I am experiencing now – would be an end in itself. That I would be so involved with the day-to-day machinations of maintaining my spot at the top of the pile that I'd literally be begging for a day off. The truth is that lately I spend most of my time wondering what the hell I'm supposed to be doing. It's gotten so bad I brought up the issue with Sarah.

'What do you mean *do*? You don't need to do anything. Just think. That's what MindCast are paying you for. That's the reason you're on the front page of half the world's magazines. All you have to do is think.'

'It's not as simple as that,' I protested. 'I don't know what I'm supposed to be thinking *about*. Surely sooner or later people are going to get bored of me thinking the same things day in and day out?'

Sarah snorted at this. 'They watched your videos for long enough, didn't they? Trust me, creating stimulating, dynamic content is the least of your worries.'

'Ouch.'

'All I mean is that people don't watch MindCast for a deep, cultural experience. You're a relatable everyman, David. That's your biggest strength. You're dependable. Inoffensive. You don't have strong opinions or outlandish tastes. You're a reassuring presence. And that's a good thing. That's what makes you so appealing to so many people. It's why vloggers are so popular right now. Before that it was reality TV. And soap operas before that. People don't want their stars to shine anymore. They want to watch lives that are just like theirs. It's reassuring. It reinforces the idea that they're normal. That they fit in. MindCast is just the next logical step. Now they get to see someone who *thinks* like them too. Someone who's not embarrassed to fret about the little things in life. What to wear. What to eat. Don't you see? Just being your usual, unexceptional self is precisely what makes you so special. It's not about entertainment. At least not in the old-fashioned sense. We're too old for bedtime stories. Besides, how could fiction possibly compete in a world this crazy? No. What we want is a comfort blanket. Something familiar we can throw over ourselves and huddle under on these cold, dark nights. That's your job David. You're keeping the world warm.'

Although Sarah sounded confident, I'm still not convinced. For one thing, the proliferation of unofficial fan-made 'highlight' videos that have started to crop up online recently suggests that people are becoming restless at watching my aimless thoughts crawl past in real-time – especially when the instant gratification of a punchily edited compilation video is only ever a click away. A single six-minute video entitled *David's Childhood Traumas* has already eclipsed the figures for videos I'd made in my pre-MindCast days. Meanwhile, there are already several compilations of my dreams that have each chalked up over fifty million views. With figures like that, it's hard not to envisage a time when people stop watching the show live altogether, and simply cut straight to the highlights.

Watching my dreams back is a strange, often underwhelming experience. While I've never been especially good at remembering them, I've always been struck by their cinematic nature, as if I spend my nights crafting surreal but basically coherent movies. Watching back my dreams on the tiny screen of my mobile phone however, I am forced to concede there is no evidence of a nocturnal auteur at work in my subconscious. Indeed, even in heavily edited form, there seems to be nothing beyond a jumble of random images and sounds shorn of all context. A surreal collage of vague visual associations, fleeting inconsequential moments from my past and present colliding to produce an incoherent art-house mess.

Still, there is nevertheless something compulsive about them. In fact, I have just opened the latest compilation when my doorbell rings.

I glance at my desktop clock, surprised. Even with the saturation of pizza takeaways in my neighbourhood, it's an impressively quick response. As I sweep back my door however, I'm greeted not by a pizza delivery person, but by a sight so bizarre that I can't immediately process it.

Standing in front of me, filling my entire doorway in fact, is a giant sheep.

Or at least, a person wearing a sheep costume.

For a brief moment I wonder if this might be some kind of elaborate promotion. An advert for a new spicy lamb topping perhaps? Then I glance down and see the gun the sheep has gripped in its hand. A gleaming, oversized revolver, like something from a cartoon. The whole scene is so preposterous I almost laugh. But then the sheep takes a step forwards and shoves me so hard in the chest that I almost topple over. Realising this is no joke, I move quickly to shut the door on my assailant. But I'm too late. The sheep has already forced its way into my apartment. Instinctively I reach for my phone, but in a flash, it is snatched from my hand and dashed against a wall, exploding in a burst of plastic, glass and microchips.

The sheep points the gun at my head.

'Go inside and sit the fuck down,' shouts a muffled male voice from behind the mask. 'If you fucking try anything I will seen you on the fucking spot. And stop fucking crying.'

'I'm speaking to you live today from the home of David Callow...'

I'm sitting in my living room, my knees curled protectively to my chest. The sheep sits opposite me, the gun cradled in his lap. On the coffee table between us, is a laptop, the MindCast app open. In the bottom corner of the screen, the view counter shows fifty million people watching.

As the sheep starts speaking, I instinctively squeeze my eyes shut. 'I swear, I haven't seen your face, man. Just take what you want and don't hurt me. Please. I won't even think about you. I promise.'

Behind the mask, the sheep lets out a long sigh. 'I want you to think about me. That's the whole point.'

He points to his chest. For a moment I'm confused. Then I spot the tiny action camera pinned to his fleece, a steady red LED indicating that it's recording.

I'm being filmed.

'I'm here today with David Callow,' he starts again. 'In order to draw attention to the gross breach of human rights committed by the head of MindCast, and David's paymaster, Xan Brinkley.'

At the mention of his name, Xan's face materialises on the screen of the laptop. Though I can't see his expression behind the mask, the sheep seems satisfied, his voice growing stronger, as if projecting from a stage.

'Over the last five years, we have watched silently as the tentacles of mass surveillance have choked away the last shreds of dignity in our offices and workplaces around the globe. Brinkley, courtesy of his hideous OptimiZer *hand-cuffs*, has single-handedly facilitated the largest theft of our personal data the world has ever seen, ensuring large corporations now have more access to where we are and what we're doing than ever before. Not content with this gross invasion, he has now taken a step towards steamrollering the last bastion of privacy that we, as a species, have left… our minds.'

'Hang on a minute,' I interrupt, unable to contain myself. 'You're here because you're mad about MindCast? But that's ridiculous. Xan isn't trying to get into your mind, or anyone else's. It's just me. I'm the star of the show. And I'm here because I volunteered to be here. Nobody held a gun to my head.'

At this, the sheep seems to snap, levelling his revolver with my temple. 'And you think it's going to stay like that? Christ, you really are stupid. Don't you remember when OptimiZer was first released? It was only celebrities who wore them back then. There was a waiting list. You had to be rich to get one. They were aspirational items. How long do you think it'll be before MindCast goes mass market? Before it's mandatory? Before we're implanting chips at birth?'

On the laptop, a newborn baby appears, his head clamped in a surgical vice, a trail of wires snaking out from the back of his skull.

'MindCast for babies? But that doesn't make any... I mean, I don't think people would want to watch that?'

'Jesus! This isn't about a fucking show. It's about data. That's all any of this has ever been about. Our lives are scraped and sifted and scrutinised more than any other generation who've ever lived on earth, including people born under the Stasi. Who you're fucking. How long you're sleeping. What brand of toothpaste you use. We're just leaking that stuff. We're *oozing* it. But all that's nothing compared to you. You, my friend, are the golden goose. The final piece of the puzzle. Thanks to that thing you've got stuffed in the back of your head, there is literally nothing they won't know. There'll be nowhere left to hide.'

I glance at the screen. The baby has gone now, replaced by what looks like a man with an egg for a head. Humpty Dumpty, his skull cracked open, the ground sticky with yolk.

'Yeah, but so what? That's the trade-off, isn't it? I get the convenience of free email or knowing how many calories I've burned at the gym or whatever and they get to know me a bit better so they can show me more relevant advertising. Sounds like a pretty sweet deal to me. Besides, I'm not a terrorist or a paedophile. Why should I care if I'm being... OW!'

The sheep leans forward and sends the barrel of the gun crashing into my jaw. My head snaps back. I taste blood. Through the smear of snot and tears I see the laptop screen has filled with a brilliant flash of white, the system over-loaded by the intensity of my pain.

'Why should you care?' he shouts. 'Why should you fucking *care*? We're talking about intelligence gathering on an unprecedented scale. Forget data mining. This is mind *rape*. The end of privacy as we know it. It's not about advertising, you idiot. It's about power. Control. Sure, the marketing men might be the first to come knocking, but sooner or later this information is going to end up in the hands of agencies whose only interest is the total suppression of your freedom. In the whole of history, no system of mass surveillance has ever existed that hasn't ended up being hijacked by malevolent forces. All it would take is one bad election, and suddenly your populist-fascist government has access to the thoughts of every single citizen in the country.'

On the screen, I see an army emerging from the white, hundreds of boots marching towards poor Humpty's broken body, crushing his shell to a fine powder under their heels.

'Resistance will be futile,' the sheep continues. 'Democracy, finished. That's why someone's got to do something now. To stop this madness before it goes any further.'

He stops talking and reaches into his bag. The gun is gone now, replaced by a bulky power tool.

A cordless drill.

He squeezes the trigger and a high-pitched metallic whine fills the room.

The laptop displays a picture: my own head in profile, my brain skewed by the steel drill bit, Xan's chip torn from my skull in a flurry of blood and bone.

The view counter shows a hundred million viewers.

Two hundred million.

As he moves closer, he begins to speak again, his voice now eerily calm. 'And now ladies and gentleman, streaming live around the world from a flat in London, the star of MindCast, and sworn enemy of freedom, justice and peace, David Callow...'

He squeezes the drill again, a wasp rasping in my ear.

On the screen, a message:

STREAMING ERROR CODE 322-1: MindCast is not responding at present. Please contact an administrator.

I scream, bite, punch, kick.

The sheep pays no attention to me, my blows bouncing off him. His hoof clamps around my shoulder, forcing me down.

'I act now in the name of The Universal Declaration of Human Rights 1948, which states that no person shall be subjected to arbitrary interference with his privacy, family, home, or correspondence...'

I squirm, spit, thrash.

It's hopeless though.

He's too strong.

'... in order to protect future generations from... buzzZZZZZZZ...'

I don't hear him finish, his voice drowned out by the relentless squeal of the drill as he grabs me by the hair and forces my head forwards.

I close my eyes and wait for the end.

Everything is happening so quickly that it's hard to make sense of what's going on. For a split second the drill touches against the back of my head, a white-hot burn flashing through me, the world lost to the scream of ruptured flesh and twisting metal.

But then it stops.

I sense the drill being pulled away.

I open my eyes.

And to my amazement I'm still alive.

The sheep has let go of me. He has turned away, the drill hanging limply by his waist, his head cocked towards the door. I follow his gaze. And now I hear it.

THUMP THUMP THUMP

The sheep half turns back to me, hesitant, unsure whether to finish the job.

THUMP THUMP THUMP

I decide to take my chance.

Running on nothing but adrenaline, I lash out a foot at the sheep's arm, sending the drill clattering to the floor. The sheep rounds on me, but at the same time my front door flies from its hinges as half a dozen armed police burst into my hallway, charging towards us.

The sheep lets go of me altogether now, diving for his bag.

Out comes the gun.

Someone starts shouting.

I dive for cover beneath the coffee table.

I bury my head in my hands as the world above me explodes into violence.

Blood and dust and smoke and noise.

At last everything falls silent. A brief pause in the carnage.

I take a chance and tilt my head, peaking between my fingers. Lying a few feet from me, I spot something familiar. The sheep's camera. It must have been knocked loose in the battle. The red light is still glowing.

It's still recording,

I move closer, picturing an unknown audience staring back at me.

Looking at me looking at them looking at me.

Hundreds. Millions.

I keep staring, squinting at the tiny gadget, until at last I am able to make myself out, a ghost reflected in the lens. Instinctively I move my hands, wiping at my tear streaked face, fixing my hair.

I take a deep breath.

Bite my lip.

And I can't help myself.

I strike a pose.

PART THREE

'So this is where you live now?'

Alice is early.

Alice is always early.

It's eleven in the morning, a full ninety minutes before she's due to be here. As ever though, she is utterly oblivious to either my irritation or the fact I am still in my dressing gown. She grins brightly, blinking as she stoops under my arm to let herself into my new apartment.

'Woah. So *this* is where Bond villains stay when they're in the city for the weekend,' she says, glancing past the ultra-minimalist décor to take in the view from my twenty-fourth storey living room, a sweeping panorama of the city below.

I shrug. 'It's pretty nice, I guess.'

'Pretty nice? It's insane. It's like Premier League footballer meets Russian oligarch. I thought the armed guards on reception were a nice touch by the way. Gives the place a real homely feel.'

There's no denying that the place is a little flashy. Apparently it was one of Xan's private residences when he first came to London. Even though I've been living here for almost a month now, I still haven't really got used to it. It's a 'smart' apartment, meaning literally everything is automated and connected to the Internet, from the shower, to the toaster, to my Bluetooth pillow – which dutifully sends a message to my phone each morning, informing me of just how little sleep I'm getting. 'A show home for the future,' Xan called it. Not that he's had the time to show me around personally yet.

After I was discharged from the hospital – where I was treated for cuts, bruises and shock, as well as providing a statement to the police – Katya arrived to whisk me off to my new, high-security bolthole, having deemed it was no longer safe to return to my old place. She explained that Xan was once again unable to break away from his commitments overseas, although this time he was kind enough to send a short video message in which he apologised for his prolonged absence and introduced me to some of the more exotic features of the apartment, which it turned out could be controlled not just by my smartphone, but by MindCast too.

In practice this means that I can be vaguely thinking about making a cup of tea and the kettle will start boiling by itself. Or I might try to recall the name of an actor from an old TV show and the credits will flash up on the nearest screen, or rather wall, seeing how almost every surface in the entire apartment is capable of transforming instantly into high-definition, cinema-sized display.

While most of these technological intrusions are welcome, there are occasions when they are less than helpful. Lights have a tendency to flicker on and off for no reason, especially at dusk, when I can't decide if it's too dark or too bright. Sometimes music blares from speakers at top volume, a single phrase or chorus repeated incessantly, mimicking a song that I wasn't even conscious of being stuck in my head. Already I have managed to destroy two separate kettles after forgetting to fill them with water and then absentmindedly thinking about tea – though admittedly, free replacements have appeared at the door within minutes. Add to this the endless parade of free takeaways (which are delivered upstairs to me by one of the guards), as well as groceries, clothes, aftershave and various other goodies sent by publicity-hungry retailers, and I have found there is pretty much no reason to ever leave this three-thousand-square-foot paradise. Which partly explains why I haven't been outside for weeks.

'You know I'm just pleased that Xan was generous enough to set me up somewhere comfortable and safe. Especially in light of everything that happened.'

Alice's smile evaporates. 'Sure. I mean, that must have been a horrible experience. The footage I saw online was just...' she trails off. 'How are you holding up anyway?'

How am I holding up?

I've heard this question more times than I care to remember over the last month.

Ever since the sheep – who within thirty minutes of his arrest had been identified on social media as Edward Samuel Corvin Jr, a twenty-two-year-old, upper-middle-class 'social activist' – had taken it upon himself to break into my apartment and hold me hostage, there has been endless online speculation about my physical and mental wellbeing. Despite issuing a number of press releases, the rumours of my faltering health continue to swirl. Of course they do. Thanks to MindCast, the whole world has been privy to the avalanche of anxiety that has consumed my life over the last four weeks. The spasm of panic every time the door knocks or my phone rings. Not to mention the recurring sheep-based nightmares that haunt the rare nights when I can actually sleep, a compilation video of which has apparently already clocked up millions of views in its own right. Yet regardless of this, I still persist with the lie that everything is fine. Better than fine. That I'm having the time of my life.

'I'm great,' I say robotically. 'Sure it's an unfortunate situation, but whack-jobs tend to go with the territory once you reach a certain level of public recognition. Besides, Edward Corvin was no Mark David Chapman. He was an attention seeker, pure and simple. You know that gun wasn't even loaded, right?'

Alice wrinkles her nose at the memory. 'I heard that. Still, some of the stuff he was saying about mass surveillance was pretty interesting. I mean he was clearly delusional, yet at the same time, some of it sounded like they were pretty valid concerns.'

'Oh, so you're siding with my attacker now? Thanks. That's really sensitive of you.'

'I'm not siding with him.'

'I'm glad to hear it. Because – and here's a spoiler alert – he's completely fucking insane. The guy is a fantasist. Worse, he's a hypocrite. Do you know that before he turned up at my place he posted a two-and-a-half-hour video manifesto where he rambled nonsensically about the imminent offline revolution he was planning to lead? I mean, come on. For a guy who's allegedly so passionate about privacy, he certainly doesn't shy away from the spotlight. I'll bet he's already penning his own autobiography as we speak.

'I doubt it. From what I hear, he still hasn't woken up from his coma yet.'

I shrug. 'Whatever. He got what he wanted.'

'A fractured skull and a shattered pelvis?'

'Fame, Alice. A little nibble of the pie. Let's face it, that's why he came after me. It's got nothing to do with some grand conspiracy and everything to do with me being high profile and easily accessible. He was hoping to get famous by association. That a little bit of my stardust would rub off on him. Well he certainly got his wish. His face on the front of every paper. His name trending globally.' I laugh bitterly. 'The irony is that, even if he does wake up, he's going to spend the rest of his life being watched. He'll be a specimen in a petri dish, locked up in a cell for twenty-three hours a day, psychologically profiled and prodded and poked, his every movement tagged and tracked and recorded on CCTV. How do you like that for mass surveillance?'

'Yes, well,' Alice says, looking uncomfortable. 'I just hope he gets the help he so obviously needs. The main thing is, it doesn't seem to have done you any lasting harm. Or your ratings for that matter.'

It's true. The extra publicity surrounding my would-be kidnapping had indeed boosted my viewing figures by a staggering amount, the red figures in the bottom corner of the screen now edging towards half a billion viewers. In fact, so popular was the siege that I've since heard the error screen I spotted during the attack was actually due to the sheer numbers of people attempting to log on, rather than an editorial decision to cut the feed. MindCast, it seems, has never been bigger.

'Every cloud,' I say, switching the subject as I lead her over to a corner of the hangar-like living room. 'Anyway, we should probably get down to it? Would you like a drink first?'

Even as I say it, I hear a tinkle in the kitchen as the fridge sends a shower of ice cubes crashing onto the marble floor.

'What was that?' Alice asks.

'Ugh. Nothing. The appliances here are set up to respond to thought command. It's pretty useful most of the time. Although on occasion the system is a little too eager to please.'

She raises an eyebrow. 'So your apartment is what? Bugged?'

'Jeez, Alice. Maybe you should go and hang out with Ed Corvin? You two can swap conspiracy theories via Morse code or something.'

She forces a smile. 'I'm fine for a drink, thanks. Actually, this shouldn't take too long. I just need to run a few bits by you and then that will be that. I'll be out of your hair for good.'

As I watch her line up her notepad and pen on the coffee table, I feel an unexpected pang of loss. 'Out of my hair? I didn't realise you were so far along?'

'Oh, come off it,' she laughs. 'You totally knew this was the last session. And you can knock off the wounded puppy eyes. You've hated every bloody minute of this process and you know it.'

'I have not!'

'Oh, and I suppose you haven't been deliberately ducking me for the last couple of months either?'

I feel my ears start to burn. 'Ducking you?'

'David, you are many things, but a good liar isn't one of them.'

'I've just been so... so overwhelmed with everything lately.'

'It's fine. I get it. You've got a lot on your plate. The last thing you need is some nosy hack poking her nose into your life. And so, the quicker we get going on this, the quicker we can call it a day.'

I watch as she reaches out for her dictaphone, her thumb hovering above the Record button.

'Wait,' I say. 'What about our deal?'

'Huh?'

'You know? I get to ask you a question before you ask me one.'

She shakes her head. Sits back. 'Fine. What's your question?'

I stammer. I haven't thought this through. 'Um… So… Will you miss me?'

'Will I miss you?'

'When the book's done.'

She shrugs. 'I'll be just glad to see the back of this whole thing, I guess.'

'You will?'

She sighs. Scrunches up her eyes. Pinches the bridge of her nose.

'I mean, don't get me wrong,' she continues. 'The book is going to sell millions. Knowing my luck, it'll probably end up being the pinnacle of my career, etched on my Wiki-pedia page for all eternity. If I can finish it that is.'

'If? But I thought you said…'

'I know, I know. But it's just so *hard*. I must be on my sixteenth bloody draft by now, and I still can't seem to get it right. I've tried rewriting it in third person, first person, a mix of both. And I've totally scrapped pretty much everything before you met Xan, seeing as that's all people are going to want to read about. No matter what though, I can't get the angle right. I just can't compete with MindCast.'

'What do you mean, "compete" with it?'

'Think about it, David. Why do you read books?'

I stare blankly at her.

'Okay, bad question. Why do other people read books then? Why do they continue to sell even though they've been surpassed by quicker and less demanding media, like TV and cinema and, dare I say it, vlogging?'

'Um… For entertainment?'

'Yes, okay. I'll give you that. People read to be entertained. To pass the time on those rare occasions when their battery's dead or they can't get a WiFi signal. But the main reason, I believe, or at least the most *important* reason people still read, is because books are the only opportunity we ever get to experience true empathy with another human being. To see the world through their eyes. To walk in their shoes. Even celebrity crap like I churn out, when it's done well, offers a unique insight, a new perspective. The chance to get inside someone else's head. But with you, the whole world's already seen inside your head. They know exactly what it looks like. What the hell could I possibly write that they can't turn on the screen and instantly see for themselves? What, in other words, is the point of this fucking book?'

I stare at her, speechless. Her eyes are shining way too brightly, and for a moment I think she's going to burst into tears. At the last second though, she collapses into a fit of giggles. I exhale.

'Sorry about that. I'm just freaking out. Don't worry, it happens at this stage with everything I write. I'll find a way to make it work. I always do. Anyway, I believe that more than answers your question?'

I nod.

She leans forward. Hits Record.

'Great. So, if it's okay with you I'm going to get straight into it. I know we spoke earlier about the Edward Corvin incident, but I just wanted to talk a little bit more about how you feel the whole experiment is going generally? The highs and lows. What has been the biggest surprise about fame, for example? And what have been the toughest challenges you've had to overcome?'

As ever, I'm amazed by Alice's instant transformation, from friend to colleague, from casual to professional. Her pen is poised in anticipation. Her tone clipped and formal. I swallow hard.

'My biggest challenge? I mean, I guess... You know what, maybe you're right. Maybe this is a waste of every-one's time. I mean, you keep asking me how I am or how I feel or what I'm thinking. But you watch the show. You *know* how I am. You know what I'm thinking.'

'Don't be like that. I'm just stressed out about the deadline. The last thing I wanted to do was make you feel bad.'

I take a deep breath. 'It's not you that's making me feel bad. It's everything. Not being able to go to the shops without a security detail. The constant fear that I'm going to be papped or attacked by mad men dressed as livestock.'

Alice nods sympathetically. 'Sudden fame can be a hard thing to adjust to. And you've undergone a major trauma lately. It's hardly surprising you...'

'It's not just that though,' I interrupt. 'It's constantly worrying about what I'm thinking the whole time, in case I accidentally offend or upset someone. Restauranteurs. Retailers. The other day I even got a text from Sarah saying Nadeem is suing me. Can you believe that? My own best friend, taking me to court. Apparently he felt that my opinion of his latest piece-of-shit cookery video was so bad that it constituted defamation. But don't worry, he's just the latest in a long line of litigious so-called friends and acquaintances. Including, surprise, surprise, my insane ex-girlfriend Ella, who is apparently in the process of issuing me with a restraining order that prevents me from thinking about her without giving her prior notification in writing. But what am I saying? You know all this already. The moment it pops into my head it's there for the whole world to see. I mean, never mind you worrying about the book competing with the show, what's the point of *me*? Why should I bother opening my mouth if everyone already knows what I'm going to say?'

There is an awkward silence as I finally finish my outburst, punctuated only by the click of various lights flickering on and off around the apartment.

Alice puts her pen down and waits, choosing her words carefully. 'But what did you expect this would be like?' she says at last. 'I mean, the fame. The constant attention.

That's what you signed up for, right? I thought this was everything you wanted?'

'And it is,' I reply. 'It's just that I wish I could get...'

'Some privacy?'

'No. I don't know. I just feel so powerless at the moment. At least when I was making videos, I had some control over what was going out. I could edit them, you know? But with this, there's no filter. I'm just constantly vomiting up the undigested contents of my brain. It's exhausting.'

'Although to be fair, there is something you can do about that.'

'Oh, right. Like go and live in a cave?'

'Well, at the very least, you could slow down and start by paying some attention to your thoughts for once. After all, we all get a choice about what we do and don't think about.'

I blink a couple of times, still not following. 'Huh?'

'Oh come on, David. I'd have thought a clean-eating self-improver like you would have been all over the whole "mindfulness" thing. Don't tell me you've never tried meditation?'

'Um...?'

With a laugh, Alice reaches for her phone. 'Here. Let's try a little experiment.'

Before she can unlock it, the nearest display panel automatically blinks on, tuned to the muted chaos of MindCast. I watch for a second, the pictures coming thick and fast, a jumbled collage flashing in and out of focus.

I'm thinking about what I am going to have for lunch.

I'm thinking about going to the gym later.

I'm also, to my intense embarrassment, thinking about Alice.

We both watch in silence as she dances onto the screen, dressed in the same tight black dress she was wearing when she visited a few months back, rather than the jeans-and-cardigan combo she's in today.

'Okay, okay,' Alice says. 'That's exactly what I'm talking about. Everything just crashing around your skull at a hundred and twenty miles a second. You need to slow it down. Take back control. Here, try closing your eyes for a moment.'

I do as she says.

'Okay now, take a couple of deep breaths. Try and clear your mind.'

I keep my eyes closed and fill my lungs. It's hard though. It feels like my brain is buzzing, new thoughts appearing like bubbles in a glass of Champagne, millions forming at once, rising to the top of my consciousness before popping.

'This is stupid,' I snap.

'You're going to have to try a little harder. People take years to master this.'

'Fine. But I'm warning you, this is a waste of time.'

I take a deep breath.

'This isn't working. I can't just *stop* thinking.'

'Stop trying to fight it then. Just relax and let the thoughts come and go. But at the same time, try and hold one thing in focus.'

'What?' I whine. 'Think but don't think? You're not making any sense.'

'Fine then. A cloud. Picture a cloud, floating through a summer sky.'

'Sure.'

With my eyes closed tight, a white cloud gradually draws into focus, rising and falling in the void in time with my breath.

In... Out...

In... Out...

Up... Down...

Up... Down...

'That's it. You're doing it, David. Keep it going.'

Very slowly I open my eyes a fraction. There on the wall, just as I'd pictured it, is the cloud, quivering slightly as it floats across a blue sky. I let my eyes fall shut again, not ready to let it go yet.

'You see?' Alice whispers. 'You can do it when you try. Just think. If you can actually learn to regulate and manage your thinking like this, you'll be able to *decide* what appears on the screen. Rather than just streaming whatever pops into your head, you'll actually have the chance to create content. It'll be like making videos again, only on a bigger scale. But first you need to keep practising so that... Oh. I guess I was boring you?'

I open my eyes. There on the screen is a sleek red convertible BMW, tearing across a desert highway. The image cuts to me behind the wheel, a pair of Ray-Ban's wrapped around my face, the wind in my hair, a smile on my lips.

'Really, what is it with you and sports cars? Every twenty minutes and it's the same, stupid fantasy. You're like a child.'

I keep staring at the screen, the glimmering BMW badge framed for a second, before the car accelerates into the distance. Almost imperceptibly, the room seems to shudder, the floor tilting underneath me, before righting itself.

'Alice, I'm not thinking this.'

'Okay. Whatever you say, car-boy.'

'No. Seriously. These are not my thoughts. I mean, now that I'm watching it they probably are. But before that, I don't know. It's weird...'

'Hey, relax. It's probably just your subconscious throwing stuff out. You said it happens all the time, didn't you? Anyway, you spend half your life fantasising about that bloody car. It must be the third or fourth time I've watched that sequence this week alone. I would have thought someone of your status would be in the position to go ahead and buy the damn thing and put us all out of our misery...'

'Third or fourth time this week?'

Around me, the room once again begins to shudder. This time it doesn't stop. It continues to vibrate slightly, as somewhere twenty-four floors below a faint, high-pitched wail begins to sound. A car alarm. A baby crying. An air raid siren.

'Screen off,' I say, though even as the words are forming on my lips, the screen fades to nothing, the hateful image of the car disappearing with it.

'Hey, are you okay? You look pale.'

'I'm fine,' I croak. 'I didn't sleep well. I'm just tired.'

A silence stretches between us. A second. A minute.

'Okay. Well, honestly we're probably just about finished here anyway.'

The high-pitched sound grows louder. I push a finger in my ear, twist it.

Tinnitus.

'You sure you're okay?'

I nod.

'Cool.' She gathers her things, stands.

I stay seated, clear my throat. 'How does it end?'

'I'm sorry?'

'The book, I mean. You said earlier you'd cut everything before MindCast. But what happens next? Where does it end?'

'Oh gosh, I don't know. To be honest, most of these books tend to follow a formula. I normally conclude with the subject looking ahead to the future, to new challenges ahead. They've won the battle but there's still a war. That sort of thing. You never want to wrap things up in too neat a bow, so that you leave room for a sequel. Most big stars have three or four autobiographies these days. As far as *your* ending though, who knows? I mean, I've got a couple of ideas, but I don't want to say anything yet. Besides, you still might surprise me.' She smiles, reaches into her bag and produces a wad of printed A4 pages. 'Here, you can have these. It's the first half. Let me know if there's anything you're not happy with.'

I scan the first few lines:

From below, the entire structure appears to be made of glass.

Ceiling, walls, floor.

A giant bubble suspended a few hundred feet above the courtyard, supported by a complicated arrangement of stainless steel beams and high-tensile wires.

A teardrop caught in a spider's web.

'It looks fine,' I say, forcing a smile. 'Thank you.'

'You think? I'm not sure. When I read it back the other day I worried the symbolism might be a little... on the nose.'

'Symbolism?'

She laughs. 'Don't worry. It's probably just me.'

Another awkward moment passes. For a second I think she's going to reach down and hug me, but then she extends her hand for me to shake. 'So, I guess this is it then. It's been... it's been interesting. I hope things, you know, work out for you.'

'Who, me?' I snort defensively. 'I'll be fine. I mean, look at this place. I'm on top of the world.'

She nods. 'You're right. You're doing great.'

We walk in silence across the expanse of the apartment, until we reach the door.

'You know if that car thing is seriously bugging you, you could always give Xan a call?' she says. 'I mean, I'm sure there's an explanation for it.'

I shrug. 'It's fine. Like you said, it's probably nothing.'

'Okay then.'

'Okay.'

We shake hands one last time. And then she's gone.

I walk back across the apartment, collapse into a sofa. The place feels even bigger now that Alice has gone. I touch the back of my head. Ever since the attack, the scar where the chip was implanted has been throbbing. The tissue tender. Under my fingers, the patch feels shiny and hairless. Almost like plastic. My ears are still ringing. I hold my breath. Beyond the endless whine of tinnitus I hear something else. The hiss and crunch of various electrical appliances triggering all around me. Lights flicker on and off. On and off. The electric juicer begins to roar, spraying the kitchen walls with pulped blood orange. The empty dishwasher switches itself on for yet another cycle.

This place is alive. Possessed.

Next to me, the screen pings on, tuned to MindCast. Always tuned to MindCast.

My thoughts splattered across the walls, five feet high.

I bury my head under a cushion and try to think nothing.

Think nothing.

Think nothing.

Think nothing.

Hours pass. Weeks.

Outside the apartment, the nights stretch to swallow the days, the congested skies shrouding the city in an interminable brown, neither dark nor light. Neither one thing nor another.

Peering down through the reinforced window of my penthouse, I am just about able to make out the twinkle of coloured lights strung between the shops below, the narrow streets churning with a snowstorm of shoppers, each no bigger than a burned-out pixel on a broken screen.

It's mid-December, only a few weeks until Christmas. Not that I'm feeling especially festive this year. There are no decorations pinned to my walls. No tree, artificial or otherwise. No chestnuts nor open fire. The security arrangements here seem specifically designed to deter visitors, and with just me around, it hardly seems worth the effort. Besides, having not left the apartment in almost a month now, I've found myself curiously detached from life on the ground. I stay away from radio, TV, social media. Like a cosmonaut floating high above the Earth, the world outside has been reduced to a vague palette of primary colours. Something to marvel at briefly through my porthole before I return to the bland comfort of my routine, to my bubble.

Most days I wake late. Midday. Early afternoon. There is a fully equipped state-of-the-art gym here, though I can rarely motivate myself to use it. In fact, I have noticed lately that my once prominent six-pack has disappeared, replaced instead by the beginnings of a soft paunch. In that sense,

I'm glad that I have no promotional work to worry about at the moment. Nothing to worry about at all, in fact. I don't even have to clean up after myself. Despite never seeing a maid, every day I get out of bed to find the apartment gleaming, the bins emptied, my laundry washed and folded. Then again, I wouldn't be entirely surprised to find the floors swept themselves.

Up until yesterday, I have spent my afternoons making notes on Alice's unfinished manuscript. It's a strange experience reading through my own recent history, one that provokes a queasy feeling, not unlike the one I get from watching MindCast. It's not that it's inaccurate. If anything, the depth of her research is formidable. Yet while the character on the page is certainly recognisable as me, at the same time it never quite tallies with my actual, lived experiences. For one thing, she clearly has literary ambitions for the book beyond a standard celebrity tell-all. Much of it is overwritten, or embellished with poetic details that somehow don't really ring true. There are also times where she has clearly been forced to guess at how I was feeling, or what I was thinking at a certain time. The strange thing about this, is that even where I spot something is wrong, I can almost feel her words erasing my original recollections and replacing them with hers, in the same way that Mind-Cast's almost-but-not-quite simulations of my thoughts end up being the final, fixed account of whatever is supposedly on my mind, my delicate memories no match for the brute physicality of the printed words or moving image.

The manuscript finishes with the attack and my subsequent rescue by the police. After that, there are only blank pages for me to make notes. As I reach the end, I'm struck by a pang of anxiety about what happens next. After all, I'm fairly sure no one will be interested in reading about me sitting around semi-dressed, growing fatter and lazier by the day. In an effort to soothe these worries, I have recently started practising the mindfulness technique Alice showed me. Hour after hour, I sit in front of one of the giant wall screens, trying my best to hold the image of the lone cloud passing slowly across the sky, all the time breathing.

In… Out…

In… Out…

I've spent so long practising that I've got pretty good at it, and now within a couple of seconds I am able to open my eyes to find the jumbled chaos that is typically displayed on the screen wiped clear, replaced instead with the image I'm currently meditating on. Having done this a number of times now, I've been able to make two interesting observations. Firstly, almost without fail, the number of viewers in the bottom right hand corner of the screen begins to plummet almost the instant I begin to meditate. While I'm not especially alarmed at the dip in numbers, I am surprised at the speed people are willing to switch off. These days I can lose half a million viewers in the blink of an eye.

The second thing I've noticed is more disturbing. Almost without fail, these meditation sessions are quickly interrupted by an extended thought sequence, the contents of which I am not only powerless to control, but that I'm increasingly convinced I haven't generated in the first place. It's not always a BMW that drives through my thoughts, although I have witnessed that scene play out in exactly the same way at least twice since I first sat through it with Alice. It's not even always cars. Sometimes an image of an ice-cold Budweiser will fill the screen, the bottle clammy with condensation, a hint of foam seeping seductively from the tip. Other times there'll be an extended sequence where I stroke the screen of a gleaming new iPhone, or else there'll be a video of me biting into a Big Mac with almost pornographic intensity, my eyes clenched in pure ecstasy as the bun splays open in slow motion to reveal the meat inside, condiment spurting through my fingers and onto my chin.

As ever, I can't be one hundred percent sure that these images do not originate in my own subconscious. Naturally, the moment I see them, I tend to immediately start thinking about the content on the screen. It also occurs to me that, as I've actively avoided watching MindCast up until now, I have no idea how long this has been going on. Perhaps this is just the way my brain works, and I've just never been aware of it before? Still, doubts remain. For one thing, these sequences always appear so suddenly, their slick production jarring in contrast to everything else on the screen, that I can't help trusting my original impulse. That these are not my thoughts. Which in turn opens up a far more troubling question.

If they're not mine, then whose are they?

In the end, I decide to take Alice's advice and ask Xan to explain what's going on. This of course is not as simple as it sounds. For days now I have tried to no avail to get through to someone from MindCast. My emails are completely ignored, and the only person I can reach on the phone is a flat-voiced receptionist who apologises that neither Xan nor Katya are currently available but promises to pass on my request for an urgent call back. In frustration, I ask to speak to Dr Khan, or even Paul, but I only ever get the same response.

There's nobody here.

I've also had difficulty contacting Sarah. It's bizarre. Over the last three years she's made it her job to micro-manage not just every aspect of my career, but my whole life. As a sort of PA, psychotherapist and life coach rolled into one, I've come to rely on her to steer me through the increasingly hectic days and nights, telling me where to go, what to wear, who to meet, what to say. Whenever there's a big news story – a terrorist attack, some political upheaval – it's always Sarah who tells me about it, breaking the issue down into instantly quotable soundbites so I that can make sense of it. Equally, when my dad had a health scare a couple of years back, she was the first person I picked up the phone to speak to.

Lately though, she just seems to have lost interest in me. After the attack at my old apartment, I didn't hear from her for a week. There was no knock at my door. No reassuring

motivational speech. No message to ask if I needed anything. Even my parents phoned me, temporarily putting
aside their issues with the show to check if I was okay. In the
end, all I received from her was a three-line text message
telling me that everything was fine business-wise and that
I should keep doing what I'm doing. Since then, I've left her
numerous essay length voicemails explaining my concerns
about the show, asking her to look into it urgently.

To stop ignoring me. To call me.

Please.

I have just left a third message for her this evening, when
my phone buzzes with a text message. I snatch greedily
for it, assuming my so-called manager has finally had the
courtesy to get in touch. The number, however, is one I don't
recognise. Opening the text, it simply reads:

Skype, 2 mins.

I swallow hard. Ordinarily I would simply write this
sort of thing off as spam. A clumsy precursor to a phishing
scam. In light of the recent attack though, the text seems to
take on a far more sinister tone. My heart begins to rattle in
my chest. Still, curiosity gets the better of me, and against my
better judgement, I find myself opening my laptop.

A few seconds later a call blinks through.

Name: Anonymous.

'Hello?'

For a moment the screen is blank. Then, gradually, an
image appears though the picture is so badly distorted that
the person on the other end is little more than a beige blur.

'Hello?' I repeat. 'I'm afraid it's a terrible connection. I can hardly make you out.'

'Hello David,' the blur says. The voice is pitched down to a robotic baritone familiar from a dozen 'real crime' shows, the same effect they use to conceal the identity of endangered witnesses.

'Who is this?' I ask, my words crackling with panic.

'Please, there's no time. Don't talk. And for God's sake don't think. Just listen...'

I squint at the screen. Even heavily disguised, there is nevertheless something disturbingly familiar about the person talking. Something about their clipped cadence, the way they roll their 'r's.

'You are in danger David,' the blur continues. 'The chip they implanted in you. It's not safe...'

'The chip? What are you talking about? Who is this?'

I'm cold, numb. Yet still there is something about the person I recognise. I rack my brain.

'Please, no questions. Just listen. Some of the components used in the M900 have been shown to produce adverse side effects in a number of studies. Amnesia... Dementia... Even death.'

'Death?'

'I have to go. This connection is not secure. Can you meet me?'

'Where?' I croak.

'At the place where this story began. Tonight, at eleven o'clock. We can talk then.'

'Where this story began? I don't understand?'

'I have to go...'

'Wait.'

As the word leaves my lips, it suddenly hits me. The person talking. It has to be...

'Katya? Katya is that you?'

The screen goes dead.

'Katya?'

Call ended.

I punch the keyboard a couple of times. Then I have an idea. I reach for my phone and bring up her original text message. I hit redial.

It rings twice, then picks up.

'We're sorry. The number you have dialled has been disconnected or is no longer in service...'

I hang up, take a deep breath.

Check my watch.

The time is nine-forty-five.

I clear my throat. Then, in a loud voice, I speak to the walls.

'Put me through to reception. I need to book a car...'

Cameras strobe and phones click. A few dozen people are waiting outside my apartment, crowding the door, tearing at my clothes, my limbs. *Over here, Dave. Looking good, Dave.* Even though it's late. Even though I deliberately turned down the offer of security so as to keep a low profile. Even though I haven't been outside for weeks. Even though my hood is pulled low over my face. Even though no one is supposed to know where I live anymore. *Over here, Dave. Looking good, Dave.* It's a mixed mob of paparazzi and super-fans, of professionals and amateurs, all of them calling my name. All of them wanting a piece of me. *Over here, Dave. Looking good, Dave.* People begging me for autographs and selfies. People begging for hugs and fist bumps. For money, for sex, for love. *Over here, Dave. Looking good, Dave.* Somebody tells me about their three-year-old daughter who's dying of cancer. She's a good kid, a huge fan of the show. Could I maybe think about them, just for a second? It would mean everything to her. *Over here, Dave. Looking good, Dave.* Someone else tells me about a new app they've developed that's going to change the world if only I could help get the word out. If only I'd think about it for a moment. *Over here, Dave. Looking good, Dave.* They're dropping bombs in Syria. Killing whales in Norway. Starving to death in Ethiopia. Somebody has to do something. Raise awareness. Spread the word. If you could just… Only a second… Make a difference… *Over here, Dave. Looking good, Dave.*

 Dave

 Dave

 Dave

 Dave

 Dave

Dave

Dave.

I fight my way through the horde to the curb, where a car is waiting for me. Prising away the fingers that have wedged between the door, I at last manage to slam it shut. I hit the lock. Exhale with relief.

'Good evening, sir. And where are we going tonight?'

I look up. The driver is smiling at me in the rear-view mirror. He's older than me. Old enough to be my dad. For a split second I dare to hope that he's never heard of me. That he has no idea who I am. There's something about his smile though. It's a little too wide, a little too intense, so that I get the sense it's only professional discretion that's stopping him saying something. From *begging* for something. Then I glance at the dash, and I know that I'm right. Because right there, propped next to his sat nav, is his mobile phone, the screen unlocked, a familiar silver logo gleaming.

'Just drive,' I snap.

'Anywhere in particular, sir?'

'Just go,' I say. 'Anywhere but here.'

The driver slips the car into gear, releases the handbrake. Accelerates. We plunge into the night.

Once I've put some distance between me and the mob, I tell the driver where I want him to take me.

'You sure about that, sir?' he asks, repeating the address back to me.

I sigh. 'Is there a problem?'

'Only I hear there's been some trouble over that way. It's just been on the news. Bad from the sound of it. Whole street's closed apparently.'

Without a word, I take out my phone.

I begin to scroll.

The mainstream news sites don't have much information yet.

Activists suspected of a major attack on MindCast HQ. Unconfirmed report of multiple casualties. This is a developing story...

Social media is already way ahead though. People are saying that the attacks are linked to last month's attempted kidnapping of David Callow. To me. People are laughing, their streams filled with jokes I don't understand. Memes featuring sheep and OpimiZer bands, the same gags repeated over again, *ad nauseam*. LOL. ROFL. Endless emojis weeping with hysterical laughter.

I try calling Sarah again, to see if she knows anything.

No answer.

I leave her a message, telling her I'm worried. I tell her about the call. About the chip. About Katya. I tell her I want to leave the show. I hang up.

I refresh the feed, keep scrolling.

New reports come in. Information. Misinformation. People are posting live from the scene. There are dark, blurry photos, seeming to confirm what many of the mainstream sites are now also reporting. That previous descriptions of a major attack are unsubstantiated. That damage to the property is minimal. That no motive has been revealed. That the perpetrator has not been identified and is presumably still at large. That there is, in fact, only one reported victim. A lone female employee.

I feel my head begin to spin.

I refresh the feed, keep scrolling.

Just then, my phone begins to vibrate. Sarah's name flashes up.

I snatch at the screen to answer it.

'Sarah? Where the hell have you been? I've been trying to reach you for days. Did you get my message? Apparently there's been some kind of attack at MindCast. Hello? Hello?'

There is a groan of distortion on the other end, my voice warped and echoing.

'Hello? Are you there?'

'David? There's something wrong with the... urgently... the chip...'

Sarah fades out again, her voice swallowed by a swell of digital noise.

'Hello? Sarah? Can you say that again? I can hardly hear you.'

I press the phone to my ear, my eyes closed, trying to make sense of the jangle of feedback vibrating from the speaker. Suddenly, her voice returns, cutting in and out, as if she's calling to me across a vast ocean, her head dipping above and below the waves, struggling to stay afloat.

'... I've found something out... in danger... Xan...'

'Sarah? What do you mean? What have you found out? Hello? Hello?'

There's a roar of static.

And then the line goes dead.

I try calling back again and again, but I only reach her voicemail.

Somewhere nearby there's an explosion of sirens.

'Some kind of attack, apparently,' the driver said. 'Terrorists, they're saying. Islamists I wouldn't wonder. Bloody fruitcakes.'

I turn back to my phone, trying to find out what's going on. I refresh the feed, keep scrolling.

A lone female employee.

No one seems to have any information. No one is naming names.

They don't need to.

I refresh the feed.

Refresh the feed.

Refresh the feed.

Another report. Breaking news. Information. Misinformation. The victim has been taken to a local hospital for treatment. She's alive but in a critical condition. Someone mentions stab wounds. Someone else mentions hearing gunshots.

Information. Misinformation.

One agency is claiming to have an exclusive. An insider at A&E. They're reporting that the victim has been badly mutilated. That their tongue has been cut out.

I think I'm going to be sick.

'Right, it's just up here, son. Looks like they've blocked off the road. They need to round up the lot of them if you ask me. Line 'em up against a wall. Make an example of 'em. I'm no racist, but...'

I refresh the feed.

Refresh the feed.

Refresh the feed.

And then, nestled between the memes and puns and links and comments, another news agency has posted another exclusive. A picture. A photograph of the victim's employee ID card, sealed inside a zip-lock evidence bag and splattered with what looks like blood.

The picture is small and out of focus, and the name on it has been redacted.

Still, there is no mistaking it.

Her sharp features. Her black hair.

Her piercing, slate-coloured stare.

It's Katya.

By the time I reach the MindCast building, most of the police have already gone, though there are still a fair few reporters loitering around, looking for a scoop. I wave away their questions with a mumbled 'no comment' and slip past the barricades and under the yellow cordon tape, offering only the vaguest of answers to the few detectives and forensic investigators who are still mopping up the scene. All of them seem to know who I am. One of them even asks me to pose for a selfie with him so he can show his kid.

At the security desk too, the guards seem relaxed. Even they seem to recognise me for once, laughing and joking with each other as they half-heartedly pat me down, waving me through when my belt buckle sets the metal detector whining.

'Have a good evening, Mr Callow.'

Over here, Dave. Looking good, Dave.

I nod, keep walking, until suddenly here I am, standing in the centre of the marble courtyard, looking up at the giant glass bubble floating high above me.

At the place where this story began.

I look around. As ever, the courtyard is completely deserted. Other than the fact it's night-time, it looks the same as it always has. There's certainly no indication of an attack or investigation. No pools of blood. No broken glass. It's as if nothing has happened. For a moment, I dare to wonder if there could have been some mistake? If all the chatter online is simply a case of hearsay, of fake news. The rumour mill working overtime. What is it they say?

Don't believe everything you read.

Then I remember the photograph. Katya's face staring back from the blood-stained ID card. And before that, the Skype call. With everything that's happened, I'd almost forgotten. That's the reason I'm here, at MindCast HQ in the middle of the night. To meet...

Who?

I check my phone.

22.58

I start to panic. What if no one shows up? If Katya's really in the hospital, then what am I even doing here? The last thing she said was that it wasn't safe to talk to me. Am I in danger? Maybe I should just leave?

22.59

I should go.

No one's coming.

I should go.

It's probably all just a big misunderstanding.

I should go.

23.00

Across the courtyard, I hear a sound. A small gasp, like air escaping from a tire. An elevator door sliding open. Footsteps echo across the empty floor as a figure appears from behind the shadow of the furthest pillar, Katya's spikey silhouette stalking towards me, the gun-shot crack of her high heels firing off the walls.

Only it's not Katya.

As the figure shuffles closer, I see that it's an elderly homeless man, his face swathed in an enormous, filthy-looking beard, his shoulders hunched around his ears, his clothes little more than rags. No, this is someone I definitely don't know. Someone I don't *want* to know. I look around awkwardly, wondering if security have spotted him yet. Surely this man is not supposed to be here. He must have stumbled in off the street during the confusion earlier, looking for a bed for the night. Somewhere warm to drink away his troubles.

Instinctively I tap my pockets, hoping for loose change or, better, something sharp to defend myself with. As the man gets within ten feet of me, he stops dead and stares at me, his face folding into either a smile or a grimace. Up close he is even more disgusting, his clothes streaked with dirt, his long hair clumped into thick, misshapen dreadlocks. He smells so bad that I can practically taste him.

I am torn between calling for help or simply turning and running, when the man extends his hand towards me. I stare at it in horror, as if he has just brandished a log of fresh excrement in my direction.

'Can I... help you?' I stammer.

'Jesus, I frickin' hope so, Dave. It's been a hell of a night.'

At the sound of his voice I recoil in shock.

I blink once, twice.

And now there's no mistaking it.

The dark circles around his eyes, the lazy Californian drawl. And there, just about visible beneath the tangled thicket of his beard, that famous scar.

'Xan?'

He smiles. Steps closer. Slides an arm around me, enveloping me in his stink.

'It's good to see you, buddy. We've got a lot to catch up on. But right now, I could do with a drink. What d'ya say?'

'You sure you don't want one?'

I watch uneasily as Xan wrenches the cap from his second Budweiser, his crud-encrusted fingers working their way around the neck of the bottle, streaking the label black.

I shake my head. 'Really, I'm fine.'

'Suit yourself.'

As we'd travelled together in the elevator – me pressed against the far wall, breathing through my mouth in an attempt to escape the smell – Xan had volunteered the details of his remarkable transformation. It had become a burden, he explained, being a public figure. The constant attention. The photos. The favours. The fame. It had gotten so bad lately that he could hardly go outside anymore. Especially while he'd been stuck over in the States, where he was liable to be harassed by rabid activists and protestors. It reached the point where he could no longer even take his early morning stroll around Central Park to clear his head. Couldn't pop down to his favourite Japanese restaurant and pick up a bento box. It was unbearable. Then he stopped washing and shaving and cutting his fingernails, and suddenly his life was transformed. He could go anywhere he wanted. Whether shuffling between the shoppers on Fifth Avenue or slumming it with the agonisingly boho in Greenwich Village, nobody blinked. He was, for the first time since he was about twenty-three years old, utterly anonymous. A complete nobody.

'It's glorious,' he explained. 'The freedom is exhilarating. These days, people actually scramble to get *out* of my way.

I can go anywhere I like. Although I guess I may need to reconsider my disguise now that I've let you in on it. After all, you never have been any good at keeping secrets...'

I kept silent as I was led through the deserted offices. Like my apartment, the lights here are automated, tracking our movements as we cut through an endless maze of corridors and stairs before clicking off the moment we pass, leaving only darkness behind us. The effect is disorientating, the usually transparent walls, floors and ceilings transformed into dull mirrors, reflecting us as we move ever deeper into the bubble. Though I didn't recognise the route, I eventually found myself back in the large room where I'd first met Xan. Tonight though, there is no sign of a guitar, the amplifier replaced with a mini fridge stocked with beers, along with two brightly coloured exercise balls.

As Xan takes a chug from a second bottle, half of which disappears in a single gulp, I at last pluck up the courage to speak. 'So how's Katya?'

Xan continues to drink, finishing the bottle. He puts it down. Wipes a lather of foam from his beard. Reaches for another.

'That's the problem with the Internet,' he says once he's got the bottle open. 'No respect for the victims. I mean the police have hardly finished dusting for fingerprints and already her name and picture are circulating online for everyone to gawp at. It's her poor family I feel sorry for. All that endless speculation.'

'So it's true then? What they're saying about her?'

Xan sighs. 'Sadly, yes. Although I hardly know any of the details yet. As fate would have it, I got back here a few hours too late. I arrived to find the police already here. Nasty business.'

'And is she still…?'

'She's expected to pull through. Dr Khan is personally treating her, so at least she's in good hands. But who ever really knows right? She's suffered an enormous trauma. These fuckin' activists are something else, man. First there's you with the sheep, and now this? I suppose you heard what they did to her? Those sick bastards. Even if she does make it, she's never going to talk again. Such a shame. She was a smart girl, too. I guess maybe they heard about the scanners and were trying to gain entry to the main building?' He pauses, takes another gulp of beer. 'Either that, or they were trying to shut her up.'

'So they're saying it was definitely an activist who attacked her?'

'Hey, I don't know the official line the police are taking, but I don't think you need to be a rocket scientist to figure out who the perp is. Or a brain surgeon for that matter.'

He snorts, drains the bottle.

'Anyway, as unfortunate as the whole situation is, I know you didn't come all this way just to talk to me about Katya. And when I say I know, well, I *know*…'

The exercise ball creaks underneath me as I shift my weight to one side. 'The thing is Xan…'

'I know what the thing is,' he says.

'You… You saw the call?'

'Oh come off it David. You *know* I saw the call. That's the whole point. I see everything. We all saw the call.' He snorts again, a single huff, somewhere between amused and annoyed. 'Anyway, I want to put you at ease and say that we have precisely zero concerns regarding the safety of the M900 chip. The materials used in both the casing and electronics are certified as one hundred percent safe to be implanted in the human body. Titanium. Stainless steel. Medical grade silicone. So you see, this talk of adverse side effects – what was it? Amnesia? Dementia? It's really nothing but scare-mongering. An attempt by some very sad and disturbed people to discredit the show. I have to say though, I'm surprised you took such, what is it that you Brits say, *bollocks,* so seriously. I mean, do you really think I'd risk everything we've been working towards just so I could save a few bucks on shoddy materials? Do you honestly think I'm that dumb?'

'No, it's just… The caller. I thought it might have been…'

Katya.

'An activist,' Xan says, finishing my sentence for me. 'Probably the same one who broke in here earlier this evening. And far be it for me to start pointing the blame stick around, but perhaps if you'd come directly to us as soon as you were contacted we could have traced the call and Katya would still have her…' He grimaces. 'Would be in better shape than she is now. But who's to really say?'

I feel my cheeks flush.

'Now, is that everything?' Xan asks.

I nod. 'Sure.'

He sighs 'Jesus, David. When are you going to learn that lying isn't your strong suit? What you really want to ask about is the adverts. Am I right? You want to know what's going on?'

'So you admit that adverts have been showing up on my feed?'

Xan chuckles, reaching for his phone. 'Honestly, David. Anyone would think you hadn't read through the terms and conditions properly?'

He pauses for a moment, scrolling, then clears his throat:

'*Section 6.2(g): User Content. Use of the SERVICE automatically grants MindCast (THE COMPANY) an irrevocable, perpetual, non-exclusive, transferable, fully paid, worldwide license (with the right to sublicense) to use, copy, reformat, translate, distribute* – and here's the important bit, Dave – *modify and/or fabricate USER CONTENT for commercial, advertising or promotional purposes. Your continued use of the SERVICE is deemed acceptance thereof…* yada yada yada…'

He kills the screen, slips the phone back into the folds of his rags.

'So in other words, yes. I admit it. As we've said all along, content is supported by the occasional advert appearing on your feed. Though, as I'm sure you've noticed, they're all super sympathetic and on-brand. After all, spots on MindCast come at a premium. Hey, don't look at me like that. You're the Super Bowl, Dave. We don't let just any old e-retailer advertise with us. We're talking about a select few. The world's biggest names taking advantage of your universal reach. Brands you can believe in on a platform you can trust. It's a perfect match.'

'But...' I say, finally managing to dislodge the words that up until now have been caught in my throat. 'But what does that mean? That you just make stuff up? The car. The beer. The burgers. You just put those thoughts in my head?'

'Made up is probably a little strong. As it happens we've found that outright fabrication usually looks a little weird. It never seems entirely real. So instead we aim to "seed" thoughts. We get the ball rolling. *You* do the rest.'

'Oh, I do the rest? Well I guess that's alright then...'

For the first time Xan's smile begins to look a little forced. 'You'll have to forgive me here, but I'm sort of struggling to see what the issue is? I mean, it's all there in the Ts&Cs. Plain as day. There's nothing untoward here. No hidden agenda. We have been open and honest with you since day one about occasionally using the MindCast platform to promote our carefully selected commercial partners. You agreed to all of this when you ticked the box and signed your name.'

I take a deep breath. Then another. 'I know that. It's just... I don't know. I need to think. I need to speak to Sarah.'

I reach for my phone, only to find a blur of coloured pixels, Xan's jammers rendering it an expensive brick.

'Do you want to borrow mine?' Xan asks gently.

I shake my head.

'Look,' he says, his voice soft and low. A mug of hot chocolate. A long bubble bath. 'Do you have any idea the costs involved in hosting a live feed twenty-four hours for an audience this size? Servers. Bandwidth. Maintenance. We pick up the tab for it all so that we can keep the service running free. And that doesn't begin to cover the six years of planning, research and development before we were in a position to launch the show. We're talking hundreds of millions of dollars. More. But we just swallowed up the costs. And then there's you. We could have charged a fortune for what you've got implanted in your brain. People would have been lining up in the streets to give us their money. But we didn't. We chose you. And it didn't cost you a penny. In fact, *we* actually paid *you*. We made you rich, dude. And it doesn't stop there. We've pumped millions into promotion, ensuring the show's a hit. And it worked! MindCast is the most talked about show on the planet. Which by default makes *you* the biggest star on the planet. We've picked up medical bills. Security bills. I've personally given you my home to live in. I don't like to blow my own trumpet, but I think we've been very, very generous. But we're not a charity, David. We can't perform all of this good work, this *magic*, at a total loss. Our shareholders would crucify us. And so, we have to be pragmatic. We have to strike a compromise somewhere. In this case, by allowing a very small number of carefully selected and artistically executed adverts onto the feed so that we can keep the lights on.'

I take a deep breath. 'Look, I appreciate everything you've done for me. And I understand the costs involved, and the need to turn a profit. I really do. It's just I think it might be for the best if I stopped for a while. It's nothing against the show. Or even the adverts. It's about me, you know? I've said the same thing to Sarah. I'm tired. Exhausted. I don't think I was quite expecting things to take off in the way they have. So much has happened lately that I can hardly think. It's not fair on the viewers. So I was hoping we could maybe arrange for me to have the chip… removed?'

Xan is silent for a moment.

'Dude,' he says at last. 'You're going to need to do better than that. You're really going to sit there and ask to give up the greatest opportunity in the history of entertainment because you're *tired*. I mean, come on.'

I shift uncomfortably, the exercise ball beginning to cut off the circulation to my legs. 'Fine,' I snap. 'It's not just that. I don't feel like you've been straight with me. You told me the show was live and unfiltered, right? Yet you're adding things in, passing them off as my thoughts. It's… It's… unethical.'

'Unethical? Really? And how is it any different to what you were doing before? Don't give me those wide eyes. You forget that I was a huge fan of your videos long before MindCast. I remember you unboxing the latest phone or console. And what about those bottles of aftershave or trainers that always just happened to be in shot. That was product placement at its finest, my friend. And I'm not judging you for it. Like I said, I get it. We're all forced to make sacrifices in the pursuit of beautiful content. Besides, the show *is* live and unfiltered. Or at least, it's nearly live. And as for unfiltered?' He smirks. 'Well, let's just say, I've seen the raw footage. And trust me when I tell you that a little bit of editing is better for everyone involved.'

'What do you mean by that?'

'What I mean is we have an entire department dedicated to flagging and censoring any, um, inappropriate content.'

'You've lost me.'

'You want me to spell it out dude? Okay, put it this way. Did you ever hear the myth that men think about sex once every seven seconds?'

Already I feel my ears begin to burn. 'Maybe?'

'Well it turns out that it *is* definitely a myth. But not by much. Judging by our controlled study of one, I'd say it's more like once every three minutes.'

My mouth is so dry I can hardly speak. 'Huh?'

Xan raises an eyebrow. 'So you're trying to tell me that in all the time that the show has been running, it never struck you as odd that there's never so much as a peek of pubic hair, despite the fact that you, my libidinous friend, have a mind like a proverbial sewer?'

'I guess I never really thought about it...'

'Oh you think about it alright,' Xan says, exploding into laughter. 'And how! You know it's not even so much the volume of thoughts that gets me – and believe me, there's a lot – but the sheer variety. The breadth of your depravity, if you will. Thin. Fat. Black. White. Male. Female. *Animals*. Is there anything that doesn't turn you on? I mean, I always thought of myself as oversexed, but next to you I'm practically a priest. Although perhaps that's a poor comparison considering the ages involved in some of your darker fantasies.'

'What?' I splutter. 'You can't honestly be calling me a...'

'Relax, dude. I'm not sure age of consent matters too much when it's just your imagination?'

'But I didn't. I've never...'

'Ah, relax. Your sickest secrets are safe with me,' he grins, slapping a filthy hand against my shoulder. 'Anyway, the point I'm making is that we have a crack team of guys whose entire job is to weed out any problematic thoughts and then stitch the visuals back together so that nobody notices a thing. And it's just as well, too. Can you imagine the complications if we just left it all in unedited? The public outcry? Not to mention what it would do to your poor parents. I mean, they practically disowned you after you let slip that Daddy was a little heavy-handed when you were a kid. How do you think they'd cope when the whole world discovers their one and only son is a sex-crazed pervert? Hell, it'd probably finish them off altogether...'

'You wouldn't... You can't...'

'And then there are the lawsuits to consider,' Xan continues. 'I mean, I know you've had a couple of legal problems of your own recently, but they're nothing compared to what would be unleashed if that stuff ever got out. It would capsize the show. And I'm not just talking about sexy stuff, either. There's the other things to think about.'

'Like what?'

'Oh, I don't know. The casual racism? And the violence. Wow, the violence definitely gets cut. There was that time you thought about decapitating your ex-girlfriend and stuffing her body into a suitcase. Sheesh, I can still remember the panic in the editing suite when you cooked up that little doozy.'

'Racism? Violence? But I never... I mean, I'm not...'

'Hey, don't worry about it. We all do it. Those dark thoughts that creep into our subconscious. Man, if somebody could see into my head... Let's just say they'd have nightmares for weeks, bro.'

He pauses, leaning closer, so that his stink fills my nose, choking me. He smells as if he is rotting from the inside.

'All I'm saying is that it's perfectly natural, man. Most of the time you're probably not even aware that you're thinking this stuff. But you are. Trust me. I mean, if you don't believe me, we could go and watch some of it now? I have to warn you though, it's pretty messed up.'

I swallow hard, trying not to be sick. 'You mean... You keep it?'

'Of course we keep it! We've got terabytes of the stuff. Petabytes of it. It's a veritable mountain of shame. Hey, don't look so worried, dude. It's perfectly safe. It's all stored offline and protected with 256-bit AES encryption. It's the digital equivalent of a nuclear blast-resistant door. No one's getting their hands on it.'

'But why keep it? Why not just destroy it?'

At this, Xan's smile drops, his eyes narrowing conspiratorially as he raises his thumb and forefinger, pressing an imaginary gun to my forehead. 'Oh, you know. We like to keep it around as insurance. Just in case you try to do anything stupid. Like leaving the show.'

He holds my gaze for a moment, a chilling look in his eye, before he snaps his fingers and collapses into peals of laughter. 'Jesus, your face! You need to learn to relax, dude. I'm joking, obviously. No, the real reason we keep it on site is that, simply put, it's safer that way. Data recovery is so advanced these days that the concept of permanently deleting stuff is pretty much a fiction. Besides, keeping your dirty linen under lock and key rather than burning it out on the street is far less likely to draw unwanted attention, wouldn't you say?'

I give a small nod, though in truth I'm struggling not to vomit.

'Okay, great,' Xan says, standing up and stretching, sending yet another wave of stench towards me. 'I'm glad this has been such a productive meeting. I think we can probably leave things there for now. I don't know about you, but I could really do with forty winks. It's been a hell of a day, and tomorrow's not shaping up to be much better. Here, I'll show you out.'

As we traipse back through the maze of glass and mirrors, Xan continues to rabbit away, churning out the latest audience records we've smashed, the latest territories we're set to conquer.

'Oh by the way, I'm not sure who advised you that meditation was a good direction to take the show, but from the viewers' perspective, it's like watching the screen saver at a health spa. You don't get half a billion people tuning in every day to watch a cloud drifting across the sky. Trust me.'

At last we make it back down to the lobby. Xan stands facing me. Even dressed as he is, there's still a hint of the entrepreneur about him. His capped teeth gleaming through his beard. His chest pushed out beneath his rags. He has the air of someone who's just closed a major deal.

'Do you need me to call you a car?' he asks.

I shake my head 'I'll be fine. I might even walk. You know, get some fresh air?'

Xan shrugs. 'Well, be careful if you do, bro. There's a lot of crazy people out there.'

He reaches out a hand for me to shake.

And that's when I see it. Just above his wrist, where his sleeve has pushed back, is an unmistakeable streak of red.

Following my gaze, Xan smiles and pulls down his shirt. In an instant the stain is gone.

I am thinking: Maybe it was just a splash of wine?

I am thinking: Perhaps it was never there at all?

I am thinking: Stop. Thinking.

We shake hands.

As I turn to leave, Xan calls out to me. 'Hey, I meant to say earlier, but now that my business in the States is wrapped up, I'll be around full-time again. In other words, you'll be seeing a lot more of me, Dave. A lot more.'

I keep walking.

I don't look back.

Outside it's begun to sleet. Fat streaks of ice pummel my skin, my breath escaping in clouds. The streets are deserted, the police having long since packed up for the night. Even the press have moved on. On to the next story, the next victim, the next witness. An endless conveyer belt of misery rolling on and on and on. The only sign that anything untoward has taken place is a lone strip of police tape, fluttering in the wind.

I pull my coat tight around me and start walking, my head bowed against the onslaught. I have no idea where I'm going other than away from MindCast.

Away from Xan.

Away from Katya.

Away from it all.

I keep trudging forwards, my face and fingers numb, my head spinning. I try my best not to think. It's easier that way. Safer that way. Instead I keep my eyes glued to the ground, watching my feet as I splash through an ocean of grey and brown.

Eventually I stop, too tired and frozen to go on. I take out my phone to request an Uber. When I unlock it, however, I see that I have thirty missed calls, all from the same number.

From Sarah.

Without thinking, I hit redial. The phone rings. Picks up.

'Hello?'

'Sarah? Can you hear me this time? I've just been to see Xan. Something terrible has happened. I need to…'

'Hello?' the voice says again, cutting me off. 'Who is this?'

'What do you mean? Sarah? It's me, David.'

Yet already, doubts are forming. The voice is wrong. Similar, but off somehow.

Too young. Too broken.

'Hello David.'

It's not Sarah.

'This is Pamela. Sarah's sister.'

And even before she says it…

'There's been some kind of an accident.'

Even before she spells it out for me.

'They did everything they could for her but…'

Her voice cracking.

'I'm so sorry to have to tell you…'

The tears, now.

'I know how much you meant to her.'

I know.

'She was always talking about you.'

I know.

'You were her favourite client.'

She's...

'I don't know how to say this, but...'

She's...

'She's...'

Gone.

Alice is early.

Alice is always early.

She's sitting in the small café where I've asked her to meet me, a small cappuccino steaming alongside her trusty notebook and dictaphone. Even though I'm fairly certain I've not been followed, I'm still careful to walk past the window three times before I finally enter. I've instructed her to take a table at the very back of the shop, and as I slip into the seat opposite her, she does a double take, as if not recognising me at first.

'Well hello, Jackie O.'

I pull back my hood and take off my oversized sunglasses, laying them down on the table. 'Funny. You know how hard it is to go anywhere with this face?'

'Okay, I'll let you off. Although, I've always thought that if you're looking to avoid unwanted attention, wearing sunglasses during the depths of the British winter is probably not the way to go about it.'

I sigh. Maybe coming here was a mistake.

'Hey, I'm joking,' she says, suddenly serious. 'I heard about Sarah. How are you holding up?'

Sarah. The official story is that she'd suffered an accidental overdose. Some kind of mix up with the painkillers she'd been taking for a slipped disc, despite the fact I've never once heard her complain of a bad back. Either way, quite how she'd managed to accidentally swallow sixty OxyContin pills is beyond me. The papers had been vague. In fact, the papers had hardly covered it at all. What few obituaries there are seem to consist of little more than reposted social media quotes from her various clients, invariably accompanied by an extremely unflattering photograph taken on a beach in Bali about nine years ago. At her sister's request, I stayed away from the funeral, her family fearful of me turning it into a circus. Since then, I've tried my best to keep busy. To distract myself. To not think. At the mention of her name though, I struggle to keep my voice steady.

'Yeah, it's crazy. I can't get my head around it.' I pause. Take a deep breath. 'I mean, we hadn't been in touch a whole lot recently. If I'm honest, we'd been drifting apart ever since MindCast took off. She was busy with the business side of things. And I've been so wrapped up in the show. It's sad. We used to be so close. Especially in the early days. I mean, she practically discovered me. The only reason I'm here is because of her. Lately though, she was different. Distant. Evasive. I can hardly remember the last time we had a proper conversation. And then, just the other day, she called me out of nowhere. Literally just before it happened.'

'What did she say?'

'I don't know. It was a bad line. She got cut off before she could tell me. She sounded weird though. Upset maybe. She mentioned finding something out. And then she was just... gone.'

Alice nods. 'It's tough. Addiction is a horrible disease. It makes you selfish. Isolates you from everyone.'

'That's the thing. I don't believe she was a...'

I force myself to stop. Change the subject.

'You know what? There's no point in dwelling on it. It's been a rough time, but I'm doing better now. Trying to stay positive. In fact I'm almost feeling... hopeful.'

Alice frowns. 'Yes, I noticed that you'd been unusually cheerful on your feed. I was a little...' She pauses, checks herself. 'I mean, I'm glad that you're managing to put such a positive spin on things. And obviously, if you need anything...'

She trails off, takes a sip of her cappuccino, an awkward pocket of silence opening up around us. I press my finger absentmindedly to the tender patch at the back of my head. It's been hurting more than ever lately, a constant burning sensation that keeps me awake at night.

'So anyway, you said you had a couple of last-minute edits for me?' she says finally, reaching for her dictaphone. 'Do you want to talk me through them?'

Without a word, I reach out and take the recorder from her.

'Hey…' she says.

'Just watch,' I say, sliding my phone across the table, MindCast open. The screen is littered with the usual cacophony of thoughts. The selection of muffins and pastries on the counter behind Alice. An unusual dog I spotted on my way over here. I close my eyes briefly, breathing deeply for a couple of seconds.

In… Out…

In… Out…

When I open them again, the screen is blank save for a single cloud, floating in the void.

'Impressive,' Alice says. 'You've been practising.'

I ignore her, doing my best to hold the image in my mind. I keep breathing.

In… Out…

In… Out…

At the same time, I fumble across the table for her notepad and pen. Taking off the cap, I write upside down, trying my hardest to work on instinct, not to read the words, not to think, not to think, not to think.

Can't talk here, I scrawl in shaky, childlike letters. *Not safe*.

On the screen, the cloud begins to flicker, my words beginning to appear in mirror image, emerging in scratchy flashes, like a brass rubbing.

'Can't talk?' Alice reads aloud.

'Shhhh,' I say, writing as fast I can.

Go to park instead.

As soon as I loop the final 'd' I take the notepad and tear out the page, ripping it into confetti-sized flakes. It's no good though. The cloud has vanished altogether now, my secret note shining brightly, the letters slithering like worms, reversing themselves so that they are almost fully legible.

Desperate, I take another couple of deep breaths, but it's hopeless. I can't get my thoughts under control. With a final glance at the screen, I take the pen, bite my lip and plunge the nib into the back of my hand as hard as I can. Even as I let out a muffled yell, I glance down at my phone, relieved to see the words on the screen consumed by a flash of white.

'Jesus!' Alice yells, staring down at the blood that is already streaming down my wrist and soaking into the cuff of my coat. 'What the hell are you doing?'

'Did you read it?' I ask, ignoring her.

'You're going to need to see a doctor,' she says, handing me a fistful of serviettes. 'Here, put some pressure on it. You could get blood poisoning or...'

'DID YOU READ IT?'.

'Yes...'

'Well then. Why are you still talking? We need to go.'

Bandaging my injured hand as best I can, I slip the phone into my pocket and scrape back my chair. As I do, scraps of torn paper flutter to the floor. Alice stoops to pick them up.

'Seriously. We need to go right now.'

She looks up at me, and for the first time I notice the terror in her eyes. For a moment I think she's going to bolt. At last she nods, sweeps her recorder and pad into her bag and, without a word, heads for the door. I slip on my sunglasses, pull up my hood, and follow her out into the street.

'Where do you think the ducks go in the winter?'

We're standing in the same deserted park we'd first visited back in the autumn. I'd hoped that we'd be safe here for a bit, especially as I'm not really sure where 'here' is. Glancing down at my phone though, I'm no longer so sure. Already the jumbled feed has recovered from the sudden burst of pain, and is currently spewing out a collage of churned mud and evergreens, interspersed with childhood kickabouts with my father. It won't be long before they start figuring out where I am.

Before *he* figures out where I am.

I look up at Alice. 'What's that?'

'The ducks?' she says again, pointing out at the lake, which today has frozen solid, the surface clouded a dull, glaucoma grey.

I stare at her blankly.

'It's a joke. A reference to… Don't worry about it. So, are you going to finally tell me what this is all about? Or do you want to have another rummage through my pencil case for more creative ways to mutilate yourself?'

'Just give me a second, okay?'

I close my eyes, begin to breathe deeply.

In… Out…

In… Out…

'Come on, David. I've already seen your party piece.'

'I said hang on.' I snap. 'I'm trying to get some privacy here. I need to talk without everyone seeing.'

Alice groans in frustration, puts her face in her hands. 'Give me a break, will you? First of all, you send me a cryptic message from an anonymous email account saying you want to meet up to discuss the book. Next, you attempt to turn your hand into a shish kebab. And then, to top it all off, you drag me to an abandoned park in the middle of winter so you can start bloody meditating. I'm freaking out here. Can you just stop talking in riddles for a moment and tell me what the hell is going on?'

'Talking in riddles?' I say. 'I spend half my life *thinking* in riddles just so I can get a couple of minutes of…' I pause mid-rant. 'Hey, I've just thought of something. The adverts.'

'Adverts? What are you talking about?'

'The car, the car. You remember, from last time we met. You said I think about it all the time?'

'You're still going on about that?'

'How often? How often?'

'David I don't…?'

'How often do I think about the car? Or the burger? Or the beer or whatever? How often do they show up on my feed?'

She shrugs. 'I don't know? Every fifteen minutes or so? It just depends. But seriously, David. I think I'm going to go. I don't think you're very well at the moment. Maybe you need to talk to someone?'

She takes a step back.

'Please,' I say. 'Just stay until the next advert comes on and I'll explain everything. If you still want to leave then, you can.'

I can still see the uncertainty in Alice's eye, the fear. But somewhere behind that is curiosity.

For the next few minutes we huddle over my phone, watching my thoughts skate and shimmer across the screen. Standing so close to Alice, I can feel the heat from her body radiating through her coat, a tingle of electricity between her arm and mine. To my horror, I involuntarily begin to imagine her body beneath her coat, her breasts shimmering with perspiration, her thighs parting...

Of course, these pictures never make it onto the screen. I picture a man in a dimly lit control room somewhere, hunched over a strip of film with a pair of scissors in his hands like an old-fashioned movie editor, a cigarette clamped between his teeth as he frantically snips away at the smut, sewing the strips back together and feeding them back into the projector. Interestingly, this man doesn't appear either. Evidently he has censored himself too, maintaining the illusion of accuracy, of transparency. No, the feed keeps on rolling without a bump, skipping flaw-lessly to another memory or thought, each one triggering another two, then another two more, like cells dividing, multiplying, growing, evolving, the never-ending stream of pictures bringing with them a familiar wave of nausea.

Just as I reach the point where I feel I can watch no more, the feed switches again. A new laptop appears, a sleek, minimalist slab of aluminium and glass.

This is it, I realise. This is my chance to speak freely. I take a deep breath and turn to Alice.

'I haven't got long, so please just listen. I'm in danger. I think maybe you are too...'

As MindCast continues to show the image of the laptop, lingering on the magnetic power cable, on the cleverly concealed USB ports, I tell Alice everything I know.

I tell her about Katya. About the Skype call. About her warning.

I tell her about Sarah. How I don't think it was an accident or suicide.

I tell her about Xan. About him admitting the adverts. About him editing my thoughts.

I tell her about him threatening me when I said I wanted to leave the show – though I leave out the part about the stockpile of sexual fantasies.

I tell her about the streaks of blood on his sleeve.

I tell her that I'm frightened.

That I'm tired of being watched.

That I can't eat or sleep.

That I need to get away.

That I need her help.

When I finish talking, Alice stares at me, her eyes wide, her mouth hanging open.

'Can you prove any of this?'

I gesture towards my phone, where the image has panned out to show me rattling away on the laptop keyboard. I'm wearing my fake glasses, my hair swept into a neat quiff. I'm concentrating, but having fun with it. I'm being super productive, but also super social, chatting to my friends online, posting hilarious pictures, reading emails. I'm a multi-tasking maverick working in synergy with this beautiful, *versatile* machine.

'I'm telling you, this isn't what I'm thinking. None of it. What more proof do you need?'

Alice raises her eyebrows. 'I don't know? It's all just so...'

'Look, I don't need you to believe me. I just need you to get me out of here.'

'Get you out of here? David, I'm just a writer. Even if I did believe you, I don't know what you honestly expect me to do?'

'But don't you see? You're the only one who *can* do something. Do you remember telling me about your brother? The one who disappeared on his stag do?'

And then, as the advert on the screen plays towards its conclusion, zooming in on the illuminated Apple logo before the screen begins to fade to black, I tell her my plan.

※

It's late afternoon, Christmas Eve. Everyone is busy. Shopping. Wrapping. Rushing. Finishing work. Getting on the road. Going home to friends, family, kids, lovers. The whole world panicking. Frantic. Not me though. I am perfectly calm. I am thinking.

Nothing.

For the last three-and-a-half hours I have been walking.

Forwards, forwards, forwards.

I am walking out of the city, heading north along Epping New Road. On my back, a rucksack stuffed with supplies. A change of clothes, a sleeping bag. A gas stove, a torch. A few packets of food, a bottle of water. Not enough that it might draw attention. Not enough to give anything away.

I keep walking.

Forwards, forwards, forwards.

The tower blocks and offices are long behind me now. Even the suburbs have thinned out, replaced by a tangle of hedgerows and skeletal trees, their branches stripped of their leaves by the whip of the winter wind. Not that I'm cold. In fact, I'm sweating, though it is probably down to excitement as much as exertion.

Because today is the day.

After a week spent secretly scheming. A week desperately trying to act normal. A week of unbelievable stress, convinced that any moment my own thoughts will accidently give me away, today my plan is finally being put into action.

Today, I am going to disappear.

The light is starting to fade now, but the road is well lit, a constant stream of traffic hurtling along each lane, their headlights dazzling, blinding, bleaching the world white. Into the city, out of the city.

Forwards, forwards, forwards.

Faster, faster, faster.

Home, home, home.

Everyone except me.

I keep to the shadows, tucking myself into the verge. My head bent low to conceal my face. Nobody stops or slows down. Nobody notices me. For once I am invisible. I try to keep my thoughts clear, my mind empty. Determined not to think anything that might give away where I'm going, what I'm doing.

All at once, my parents' faces flash involuntarily through my mind. How worried they'll be when the papers report that I'm missing. How disappointed they'll be when they discover the truth. That I'm a coward. That I ran...

I force the thoughts out of my head, working to keep my breathing slow, steady.

In... Out...

In... Out...

I picture blue skies.

White clouds.

I picture anything but the plan.

Wary of GPS tracking, I have left my phone at home today, so I'm unable to check how many people are watching me right now. Over the last few days, the number of viewers has dropped slightly, people too busy with Christmas to spend their time staring at MindCast. Still, there are those who refuse to look away. Those who don't stop, even to blink. Thousands. Hundreds of thousands. I feel them crowding around me, leaning in and peering down. Suffocating me.

Watching, watching, watching.

All it would take is for one of those people to latch onto one loose thought, to put the pieces of the puzzle together and…

I keep walking, breathing. The traffic like a buzzsaw beside my head.

Forwards, forwards, forwards.

Blue skies, white clouds.

Nobody stops or slows down. Nobody notices me.

Not yet.

It was difficult to know how much to tell Alice. I was terrified of giving myself away. Or of her knowing so much that it would put her at risk. In the end, I stuck to the basics, the bare bones, leaving her to work out the details for herself. The less I know the better.

Talking in riddles, thinking in riddles, I told her I'd like her to speak to her brother. The one who was recently married. The one who was recently kidnapped.

The one who was taken and dumped in the middle of nowhere.

I asked her to find out the name of the company who carried it out.

Talking in riddles. Thinking in riddles.

I asked her if she was following me.

I think so, she said. I think so. When, though? And where?

Christmas Eve, I said. On Christmas Eve I'm going to walk to Epping Forrest. I'm going to walk there alone. Everyone will be busy then. Shopping. Wrapping. Rushing. If a group of unknown men in an unknown van was to drive past and pick me up, well who knows? Maybe no one would notice?

Did she understand? I asked. It's important she understands.

Talking in riddles. Thinking in riddles.

I understand, she said. But are you sure?

I'm sure, I said. I don't have a choice.

But where will you go, she asked?

That's the beauty of it, I said. I have no idea.

The middle of nowhere, I said.

Alone, I said.

Alone.

Around me the evening turns into night. The winter wind keeps whipping. The traffic keeps hurtling. My t-shirt sticks to my chest. The straps of the bag cut into my shoulders. My feet ache and my stomach rumbles.

I keep walking.

Forwards, forwards, forwards.

Nobody stops or slows down. Nobody notices me.

Not yet.

I keep breathing.

In... Out...

In… Out…

Blue skies, white clouds.

Anything but the plan.

And then. Somewhere behind me. A sound. An engine easing off. The squeak of brakes in need of oiling. A side door sliding open. The sound of unknown men in an unknown van. The sound of salvation.

At the last minute I turn.

That's when I see him. My guardian angel in a black balaclava. He reaches out, grabs me by the arms. I offer no resistance. The passenger door opens and more men jump out and take me by the legs. I smile, lean back, let them take my weight as I am lifted, up, up, up. As they begin to carry me back towards the van.

'Thank you,' I say. 'Thank you.'

'Shut up,' says a man.

'Get in,' says another.

I am shoved roughly through the open door, onto a waiting mattress. They slip a plastic cable tie around my wrists, even though I have no intention of escaping. Even though I'm happier than I can ever remember being.

'Thank you,' I say again. I start to cry. 'Thank you.'

'Go, go, go,' shouts one of the men, thumping the side of the vehicle.

I take one last glance at the dirty December sky, before the door slams shut behind me.

Before the world goes perfectly, beautifully black.

PART FOUR

For a long time, I lie on my back in the dark. As we drive, I listen to the oscillating whine of the road as it unwinds beneath me, the changes in frequency indicating different surfaces and speeds. At first, I'm wary of paying too much attention to the direction we're travelling. I don't want to create a mental map that might give me away. Within a few minutes, however, I have totally lost my bearings. The vehicle seems to lurch in endless circles, until I can hardly tell up from down, let alone left from right. In the end, I give up and go to sleep. I dream that I'm an astronaut, untethered from my spacecraft, tumbling through the cold void of space as the Earth grows smaller and smaller behind me. Lost. Alone. Adrift.

I wake to the rasp of the side door being wrenched open. For a second I'm unsure where I am, even as a pair of strong arms hoist me up from the mattress. My own hands are still bound and I'm unable to break my fall as I'm thrown from the van onto the cold gravel outside. I lie there, sprawled face down, the taste of blood in my mouth. Moments later my rucksack crashes down beside me, before the men retreat back to the van. Doors slam, and the engine splutters to life, bathing me briefly in the yellow spill of headlights.

'Hey!' I call, my words hampered by a rapidly swelling bottom lip. 'Hey! What about my hands?'

There's no answer though. Only the spin, grip and crunch of rubber as the van jerks forwards into the night, leaving me in a cloud of diesel fumes and dust.

'Hey!' I yell again. 'Wait!'

It's too late. Within a few seconds, the twin points of the van's tail lights have retreated into the night, the growl of the engine growing fainter and fainter, before it's lost altogether in the wind.

It takes me a while to clamber to my feet. The plastic cable ties seem to have drawn tighter while I slept, and are now biting into my wrists. I wince in pain, rolling first onto my side, then to my knees, before I finally manage to stand up. My head swims. When the world comes back into focus, I look around. It's dark. Darker than I can ever remember it being in the city, the only light coming from a faint sliver of moon. Squinting, I see the road is no more than a track. Thick patches of weeds sprout between loose chunks of gravel. Rising up on either side, a dark tangle of woodland blocks my view, reawakening some ancient, childhood terror. Wicked witches. Big bad wolves. Without the constant drone of traffic to block it out, the night seems to fizz with activity. The trees above me groan in the wind. Somewhere nearby I hear the thump of falling branches. The crunch of dead leaves in the breeze. The pad and scratch of unknown paws.

Don't panic, I tell myself. *This is what you wanted.*

And even if it's not, what's the alternative? To crawl back to Xan on my hands and knees? To end up like Katya? Like Sarah?

A solitary hoot rings out from the woods. I decide I'd better start moving. With some difficulty, I manage to hook my thumb under the loop of my bag. I straighten up. Take a last look over my shoulder. Then I start walking, moving deeper and deeper into the night.

I've been on the road for around twenty minutes when I realise my water bottle has leaked. Having already tripped over several times, I stop to try and fish the torch from my bag. That's when I make the discovery. Holding the bottle to the sky, I can make out a small crack in the plastic. I curse to myself. Though I wasn't particularly thirsty when I'd stopped, I'm suddenly parched. I begin to panic.

I'm all alone in the dark with nothing to drink. I don't know where I'm going and I don't know what to do. I've made a terrible mistake. I want to go home…

I wallow in self-pity for a while, until it occurs to me that half a billion people are still out there, watching me. I try to imagine what they might be seeing on their screens right now. What they make of my attempt to escape. Are they laughing at my ineptitude? Or do they feel sorry for me? Then something else occurs to me. Perhaps I'm simply boring them? Right now, they're probably switching off in their millions. Tuning in to a new distraction. A new show with a new star. The thought makes me feel strange. As desperate as I am to get away from Xan, I still can't get used to the idea of no one being interested in my life anymore. After all, if nobody's there to watch me, what's the point in doing anything in the first place?

In order to take my mind off this increasingly bleak line of thinking, I force myself to focus on the present. To make a plan. First things first, I decide to take stock of my supplies. Though the cable ties make it awkward to manoeuvre, I eventually manage to empty the contents of my rucksack onto the road. Almost everything is soaking, including my spare clothes and sleeping bag. The torch isn't working either. When I unscrew the head to check the battery, water spills onto the dirt. I toss it aside, along with the bottle, before repacking the bag as best I can.

Then, in the absence of a better idea, I once again begin to walk.

The hours trickle by and the night disappears, the first rays of sun streaking the morning sky purple and pink. The road has petered out altogether now, leaving nothing but frozen mud beneath my feet. The trees either side have gone too, replaced by low hedges and stone walls, with gently rolling fields beyond them. At one point I begin to plot a radius around London, trying to work out where I might be, before I catch myself. The less I know the better. I keep going, my breath billowing before me, tears welling up in the corners of my eyes. *Something will turn up soon*, I tell myself, though I'm not sure I really believe it. Like Xan says, I've never been any good at lying.

At some point, it occurs to me that it's Christmas Day. Not that it really means much to me anymore. I'm not religious, and presents don't seem to carry the same allure now that I tend to instantly receive everything I wish for. Nevertheless, I find myself thinking about my parents. No doubt they'll be awake by now, perversely early risers that they are. Perhaps Mum will have already tried to call me, only to leave some rambling, nonsensical voicemail. The last few Christmases, I've gone out of my way to avoid visiting them; something about their tired decorations and fading plastic tree that's just too depressing for words. I guess it's ironic then, that this year it was them who'd made the excuse, Mum sheepishly explaining that they were planning on having a 'quiet one' and that it would be better if I stayed away. *Fine*, I'd snapped. *I have other plans anyway.*

What I wouldn't do to be there today, though. To be warming the back of my legs against their antique two-bar electric fire. To choke on a forkful of overcooked turkey. Or to quench my thirst with a glass of under-spiced mulled wine.

Thirst.

With each hour that stutters past, I become ever more aware of the lack of water. My throat is dry, my tongue fat and swollen in my mouth. Twice I've stopped to delve back into the damp rucksack, ravaging my meagre supplies in an attempt to find relief. It's no good though. The dry cereal bars and potato crisps I've packed to sustain me prove almost impossible to swallow, instantly turning to sawdust in my mouth. After each one I force down, I'm even thirstier than before.

The sun is fully up now, steam rising from the empty fields as if a fire is burning just below the surface of the world. Even so, it's bitterly cold. While my coat is thick, I've forgotten my gloves, and the tips of my fingers have turned bright red. Unable to put them in my pockets, I lift my stinging digits to my lips and blow steadily on them, dredging up a warm breeze from deep inside my chest.

As I stagger on, it occurs to me that I haven't seen a single sign of life since I started walking. No cars have passed, and there's not a hint of traffic on the wind. There are no farms. No houses. No lamp posts or telephone poles. And though the air is filled with the sweet-sour stench of fresh manure, the fields remain resolutely empty of animal life.

Again, I wonder where the hell I am, before I'm swamped by exhaustion. My thoughts slow and fuzzy. My legs concrete blocks, each step a painful battle against gravity.

Yet still I press on. Forwards, forwards, forwards. Into this desolate Christmas Day. My muscles screaming. My extremities stinging. My mouth like a desert.

Forwards, until there isn't a single thought left in my head.

Forwards, until my vision begins to flicker.

Forwards, until eventually I just stop.

I stand there for a moment, alone under the freezing blue sky.

Tottering.

Teetering.

Unable to muster the message to make my legs move. For a while it seems as if I will collapse. As if the slightest breeze will be enough to knock me down.

A falling branch.

Dead timber in an empty forest.

But then I tilt my head.

On the other side of the low stone wall is a huge field, separated by a thorny hedge. There, something catches my eye. A slash of silver, glistening in the light.

With my last reserve of strength, I force myself to start moving again. I scale the wall, one leg then the other, then hobble towards the light.

Forwards.

Forwards.

Forwards.

The cable ties around my wrists make it difficult to nego-tiate the hedge, a million tiny barbs hooking and tearing at my flesh. At last though, I push my way through.

And then I pause in amazement.

The stream is shallow but fast-moving, coursing its way along a bed of smooth, grey rock. Seconds later, I drop to my knees, burying my face in the water. It's so cold it steals my breath. I don't care. It tastes sweet and clean. It tastes like hope. I drink and drink, until my stomach is so full it begins to ache, bulging over my belt like an overinflated tire. At last I lift my face, rolling back onto the grassy bank to rest.

And that's when I see it.

A little way upstream, in a slight dip that keeps it hidden from the road, is a small house.

The tiny building is a ruin. Four moss covered stone walls propping up a ramshackle slate roof. A single room with no windows or door. There's something oddly familiar about it. Then it dawns on me. The cottage looks almost exactly like a derelict shepherd's hut I once discovered as a kid, while walking with my parents in Scotland. Back then, the building had seemed ominous somehow, standing all alone at the bottom of a craggy valley. I still remember Mum's dire warnings that it could collapse at any moment when I threat-ened to explore inside.

Today, however, I don't hesitate.

Stepping through the open doorway, I inhale deeply, sucking in a thick musk of damp and decay. The place must be at least a hundred years old. Perhaps even older. As my eyes adjust to the gloom, I see the floor is a mass of grass and brambles, nature having long ago reclaimed this place as its own. Overhead, rotten beams balance precariously, large rectangles of blue visible through the shattered slate. It's not much warmer in here than outside. And it will no doubt leak when it rains.

I let my bag drop to the floor. The sound sends a fat woodpigeon erupting from the rafters, making me jump. The bird beats a panicked circle until it eventually finds a hole in the dilapidated roof and disappears.

I smile. It's the first animal I've seen in days. In months maybe.

I decide to take it as an omen.

For now at least, the hut will do.

For now, this will be my new home.

Once I've regained some strength, I begin clearing a space to sleep. With my hands still tied, it's a difficult task. At first I'm limited to kicking away at the thick tangle of vegetation, a slow and energy-sapping way to work. After a while however I uncover a number of rusting farm tools buried beneath the knot of nettles, including what looks like an ancient scythe. Though the blade is dull, through a mixture of friction and brute force I eventually manage to wrench the cable ties apart. Afterwards, I stare down at my mangled hands. They're almost unrecognisable. The scar from where I gouged myself with the pen is fringed with an ugly yellow crust. Meanwhile, each wrist is ringed with a dark red bracelet. I rub at the raw skin. Flex my aching fingers. Make a fist. *They'll heal*, I tell myself. *It'll take time, but eventually they'll be even stronger than they were before.*

I get back to clearing the floor.

By the time the evening rolls around, my t-shirt is soaked with sweat and my hands and arms are flecked with cuts. Still, it's a job well done. Leaning against the wall outside, there is now a huge pile of brambles, while the floor inside is raked smooth. Choosing a spot at the far corner of the hut, where the roof is least damaged, I roll out my sleeping bag. Then, very carefully, I take the scythe and use it to gouge a number of lines into the bare earth, dissecting the hut into three imaginary areas. Bedroom. Kitchen. Living room.

Who needs a penthouse?

As the days go by, I gradually begin to adjust to my new life. Every day I remind myself there is much to be thankful for. I have shelter. Fresh air. As much water as I can drink. Every night I use the camping stove to light a small fire in the 'living room', having managed to clear decades of detritus from inside the old stone chimney. It's not just these physical comforts I'm grateful for though. In some ways, I feel calmer than I have in months. Perhaps ever. Not that I've bothered with any of Alice's mindfulness exercises recently. In fact, since leaving the city I haven't felt the need to meditate at all. Rather, I find the simple day-to-day tasks are enough to occupy me fully. Gathering firewood. Rinsing my clothes in the stream. Sweeping the floor of the hut. By immersing myself in these activities, I find there is little time to be anxious about the life I've left behind.

Despite this progress however, there is still one problem that increasingly threatens to drown out everything else. Food. I've long since finished the last few mouthfuls of my supplies, and since then the hunger pains have grown steadily worse. Back in the city, I'd regularly undertake day-long fasts as part of various detox diets. However, the bad breath and headaches I'd experienced whilst skipping the odd meal are nothing compared to the hollow cramps that now gnaw into my every waking thought. Yesterday, and again this morning, I set out on a long, circular walk, hoping to find something, anything, I could put in my mouth. Hours later I returned empty handed, having seen nothing but deserted fields.

Lying curled on my sleeping bag, I am forced to admit that I won't be able to hold out for more than a day or two longer. That unless something changes, I will soon have to leave the hut. Though what will become of me then, I have no idea.

Another day passes. Then another. It's now five days since I last ate anything. I'm increasingly weak. Strange colours and shapes float across my eyes, while my ears ring almost constantly. Though I know I should keep looking for food, I can't seem to motivate myself to get up from the sleeping bag. These days, the furthest I go from the hut is down to the stream, where I suck up mouthful after mouthful of water in an attempt to appease my aching belly.

Some nights, I dream of tucking into a hot meal, only to wake up anguished, alone on the cold, hard earth. In moments like this, I'm capsized by dark thoughts, as I see with a searing clarity what a mistake it was to come here. To think I could survive all alone, away from the life support machine of society. Everything I had, gone. Squandered. And for what? My principles? My ego? To think of all that I've willingly given up. Riches. Fame. Yet what good is any of it out here? Money means nothing when there are no restaurants or shops to spend it in. And having the world's most recognisable face doesn't get you very far when there's no one around to see it. The days of simply imagining a freshly baked pizza only to have it materialise at my doorstep seem a very long time ago.

Lately, I've been considering the idea that I'm being punished for something. That someone is watching me, taking active pleasure in my suffering. Like a kid torturing an insect. My wings and legs plucked away. My body crushed, viscera splayed. I'm not talking about God.

Or who knows, maybe I am talking about God. Either way, I can't escape the feeling that all this hardship is payment for something. A twisted sort of revenge. Not just for abandoning MindCast. For running away. No. It goes back further than that. Deeper. In my exhausted mental state, I see now that I was doomed from the very first time I picked up a camera and pointed it at my own face. It was at that moment that something intractable was set in motion. A journey, taking me all the way from my bedroom to this hut. From a buoyant beginning to this starving, miserable end.

And make no mistake, this is the end.

For even if I was to give up now. To throw myself on Xan's mercy and pray for him to come and rescue me, how would he find me? Even I have no idea where I am.

For the thousandth time since I've been here, I wish that I had my phone with me so that I could get online. If only for a minute. For a second.

My kingdom for a search engine.

Because worse than even the loneliness and hunger are these nagging questions I carry around in my head from morning until night. Questions for which there are no easy answers.

Where am I?

What should I do?

How long does it take to starve to death?

The next evening, I'm lying in my hut, trying to keep warm. These last few days, I've been too tired to even get up and gather firewood, making do with short blasts of the camping stove whenever the cold becomes too unbearable. Swaddled in my sleeping bag, I suddenly become aware of a noise in the living room. At first, I put it down to delirium. An aural hallucination brought about by lack of food. I've had a few of these recently. Phantom ringtones. Email alerts. Fake vibrations in my pocket. I've even imagined I can hear my mother's voice, calling my name. *David*, she says. *Come home. Come back to me.*

This is something different though. More insistent. More real. A faint scratch-scratch-scratching, coming from somewhere inside the hut. At last I manage to rouse myself, crawling across the dirt to investigate. With daylight already fading, it's difficult to make out much. After a while though, I realise the sound is coming from somewhere behind the stone chimney. Cautiously, I poke my head into the small fireplace. Seconds later I leap back in fright as something dives towards me, a thundering blur of green and grey feathers.

Once I get my breath back, I creep forwards again. This time I see clearly the source of the noise. Somehow, a fat woodpigeon has wedged itself into the narrow chimney breast. At the sight of me, the pigeon once again begins to beat its wings. It's hopeless, though. The bird is completely stuck. For a moment, I consider how I might go about freeing the poor animal. Then I think back to that afternoon with

214

Nadeem, all those months ago. Back before the madness of MindCast. The Chicken Nugget Challenge. Even if we hadn't actually managed to go through with it in the end, we'd still watched hours of videos on the subject.

I look again at the animal, its yellow eyes staring back at me. Even with its puffed-out breast, there doesn't look to be much meat on it. Still, it's better than nothing. Besides, what is it that Nadeem had said?

It's as simple as wringing its neck.

In the end, the killing is worse than I could have imagined. While I'm able to recall a surprising amount of information from the videos, nothing could have prepared me for the grisly reality of the act. Once I've managed to free the flapping bird from the chimney – a traumatic experience in itself – I place the back of its head between the crook of my thumb and forefinger. I take a deep breath. Then, with as much force as I can muster, I pull down sharply, breaking the bird's neck. To my horror, it continues to thrash for a good minute, even as its head lolls limply to one side, until at last it falls still.

Preparing the animal is not much more fun, especially as without a knife I'm forced to improvise with a sharp stone I'd retrieved from the river. As I make the first clumsy incision in the bird's chest, working my fingers inside its ribcage to remove the slippery mass of entrails and organs,

I think back again to the afternoon in Nadeem's flat. What a relief it is not to have the pressure of staring into a camera, I think. Not to have to explain every step out loud. To worry about lighting, or sound, or having something funny to say. To not care about the state of my hair.

Instinctively, I reach up and touch the tender patch at the back of my head. It's been less sore lately – so much so that I'd almost totally forgotten about it. Tracing my finger across the shiny crescent of the scar, I think about the people who are still watching. At home. At work. In their cars. I realise I've barely given a thought to them either. After months of anxiety, I'm no longer consciously attempting to be entertaining, or censor things I might previously have considered inappropriate or controversial. I could be losing a million viewers a minute and it wouldn't matter. I simply don't care what they think of me anymore.

At last the job is done and I use the little camping stove to cook the few slivers of meat as best I can. Fearful of poisoning myself, and without oil or seasoning, the finished product is by turns burnt and bland. Even so, it tastes of victory. Reclining back on my sleeping bag, already feeling a little stoned from the first food in days, my mind drifts towards my immediate problems. The gas bottle on the stove is beginning to feel dangerously light. Even used sparingly, it probably has a couple of days left in it at most. There is also the ever-looming issue of food. Realistically, how many more woodpigeons can I expect to land in my lap? And then there's…

I force myself to stop. There will be plenty of time later to worry. For now, I will just lie back in the afterglow of this small meal. For now I will just be thankful for this reprieve in the unending misery, no matter how brief it may be.

The next morning, I awake to find I have a little more energy than usual, the light-headedness that has plagued me for days having temporarily receded. Leaving the hut to wash and drink, I find that it's also slightly warmer outside than it has been lately. The sun is shining, and the sky is the exact shade of blue that used to represent 'astonishment' when MindCast first started. I take it as a sign.

Once dressed, I pack my scant few possessions into my bag. I can't stay here any longer. Glancing around the hut one last time, I can't help but feel a pang of sorrow for the dirt floor and stone walls and broken roof. As basic as it is, this place has kept me safe and dry. In many ways, it has felt more like home than anywhere else I've ever lived. Still, it's time to go. Either I leave today, or I don't leave at all.

It isn't until after I've set off that I realise I still have no real idea where I'm going. In the end, I decide to follow the gently sloping hedge that lies directly behind the hut, figuring if I can get to higher ground, perhaps I'll be able to get a better lay of the land.

Hours pass, the sun tracking slowly east to west across the astonished sky. By now I have stripped down to my t-shirt, which clings damply to my chest. My early morning enthusiasm has long since waned, replaced by a familiar hollowness. My limbs aching, my mouth dry, my vision shaky. Despite climbing continually upwards since leaving the hut, I am yet to spot anything but deserted farmland. No cars. No buildings. No planes in the sky. Again I wonder where on Earth I am. Was it possible that I'd slept for longer than a few hours in the back of the van? Could they have dumped me in a different country altogether? None of it seems to make any sense.

I decide to break for lunch. Not that I have any food to eat. I don't even have any water with me, having nothing to carry it in. Still, I have the feeling that if I don't sit down soon, I may fall. Spying a large, flat rock jutting out ahead, I let my bag drop to the grass and collapse onto my back, my hands cushioning my head.

Staring up at the sky, anxiety swarms my mind as I try to figure out what I'm going to do next. I've already walked too far to make it back to the hut before nightfall. Besides, even if I had the energy, I'm not convinced I'd be able to find it again. And if I can't, what then? Where will I sleep? What will I do about food and drink?

Gradually, my thoughts begin to slow, the spiralling panic draining away, as if someone has pulled a plug in the back of my head. For the first time, I notice a small, fleecy cloud trailing slowly across the otherwise unblemished sky. I smile. The more I stare at it, the more it begins to resemble the imaginary cloud I used to picture while meditating. More out of habit than anything else, I take a couple of slow, deep breaths:

In... Out...

In... Out...

The cloud keeps drifting across the sky, oblivious to me and my struggles far below. I keep breathing, willing the cloud to speed up.

In... Out...

In... Out...

I watch in amazement as, almost imperceptibly at first, the cloud begins to obey my command, its pace quickening as it intersects the sky. This time I actually laugh out loud. 'Very funny,' I say. 'So I'm God now?'

It's been so long since I've spoken to anyone that my voice startles me. It sounds small and frail, lost amongst the vast expanse of the natural world. It certainly doesn't sound very God-like. I return my attention to the cloud, willing it to move faster. This time it responds immediately, sliding smoothly across the sky, as if pushing a tiny white bead along an abacus.

My heart begins to beat faster, a cold terror gripping me as I realise that it's finally happened. That I've lost my mind.

'Okay, okay – you can knock it off now,' I say.

Again, the cloud reacts instantly, freezing on the spot where only seconds before it had been racing through the sky towards the horizon.

Around me, the breeze drops away, so that the only sound I can hear is the faint ringing in my ears.

'Backwards,' I say at last, my voice no more than a murmur.

I watch in horror as the cloud complies, beginning to retrace its path, moving back the way it came.

'Stop,' I say.

Again the cloud stops.

I stop breathing.

This time I don't say a word. Instead, I simply reach out my hand, so that it's silhouetted against the sky. Then I wrap my thumb around the tip of my middle finger.

I take aim and flick.

The cloud rockets across the sky, disappearing beyond the horizon. Seconds later it reappears behind me, as if having looped around the Earth. Gradually it slows down, rolling to a rest in the same spot it started in.

I jump up. My mind racing. Heart hammering. I want to run from this madness. Yet I can't tear my eyes from the sky. This time I stretch both arms high above me, framing the cloud with my fingers. Then I clap my hands together. The cloud immediately fragments, turning to a powder that sprays between my fingers in a fine mist. When I open my hands to look, the cloud has vanished altogether.

Not finished, I scan the sky for another target. By now I have stopped panicking. I have abandoned myself to insanity. Tilting my head, I aim a lazy swat at the sun. Just like the cloud, it tumbles across the sky, turning over and over like a golden bowling ball. As it moves, everything becomes dimmer, until the sun too plunges out of sight, and the world falls dark. Stars appear, peppering the black with points of white, as somewhere behind me the moon rises, tumbling gently into focus. Grinning, I flick out my hand again, scattering a constellation of stars, before lashing out at the moon, sending it reeling away as once again the sun rises to the east, the sky flooded with daylight.

Let there be light... and at once there was light.

It goes on like this for a while as I bat lazily at celestial bodies, the sun and moon switching places faster and faster. Day becomes night becomes day. Weeks and months whiz past in the flicker of an eye, until at last I grow bored of the game.

At which point, I reach up and tear the sky in two.

And then suddenly I'm not standing in a field anymore. Rather, I am streaking like a human-comet through time and space. Backwards, backwards, backwards. Stars and galaxies unravelling in a cloud of hydrogen and helium as I hurtle backwards, backwards, backwards. Subatomic particles disintegrating into photons, neutrinos, quarks. Everything coming unstuck. Backwards, backwards, backwards. Back towards the very conception point of the Universe. Backwards, backwards, backwards, until at last a blast of white heat, of pure energy, strips my mind from my body. Dematerialises me. And suddenly I am nothing.

Nowhere.

Eternity passes in an instant.

Eventually I become aware of something.

All around me. Through me. In me. *Is* me.

The fabric of everything.

It's a pattern, I realise. A code of some kind.

I squint.

And now I begin to recognise the shapes. A familiar system of dots and dashes from a world 13.8 billion years from now.

Marks on a page. Black against white.

And then, all at once, the pattern slurs into focus:

Noughts and ones.

Noughts and ones.

Noughts and ones.

01000001 01101100 01101100 00100000 01110111 01101111
01110010 01101011 00100000 01100001 01101110 01100100
00100000 01101110 01101111 00100000 01110000 01101100
01100001 01111001 00100000 01101101 01100001 01101011
01100101 01110011 00100000 01101010 01100001 01100011
01101011   00100000   01100001   00100000   01100100
01110101 01101100 01101100 00100000 01100010 01101111
01111001 00001010 00001010

I open my eyes.

PART FIVE

Blink.

I'm awake.

At least, I think I'm awake. My mind is racing so fast that in truth it's hard to tell. I look around wildly, trying to take in my surroundings. Trying to latch onto some detail that will unlock what is happening to me.

The fields are gone now. So is the sun and the moon and the sky. I am standing alone in a small box room, the ceiling, walls, floor all made of mirrored glass. There I am, reflected in every surface, staring back at myself.

Hello, David.

Only my reflection doesn't make any sense.

While I was in the hut, I'd lost track of what I looked like. There was no mirror, no phone. The stream was too shallow to provide anything but the faintest blur of my outline. Even so, I was still vaguely aware of how dirty and unkempt I'd become in the last few days and weeks. Black filth was crushed into my fingernails and palm lines. My clothes were encrusted with grass stains and dark splotches of pigeon blood. Recently, I'd also become aware of how long my beard was getting, a thick sprouting of bristles around my jaw line that often left me scratching my face deep into the night.

Looking at my reflection now, however, I'm confused to see how clean I am. Gone are the stains from my clothes. No mud. No blood. There's no sign of a beard either, other than the light shadow of a two-day stubble. I hold up my hands, confused by my sparkling cuticles, before something else catches my attention. Lying crumpled in the far corner of the room is my sleeping bag, rolled out and looking recently slept on. Nearby is my rucksack, my spare clothes spilling from the top. I start to walk towards it, then stop. On the other side of the room is my camping stove, along with a small frying pan. And there, in the very centre of the room, equidistant between the two, is a small pile of rubbish. The empty packets of food look suspiciously like the supplies I'd finished eating days ago.

I struggle for breath, my airway seeming to collapse in on itself. The room is laid out in the exact order that I'd set up the hut.

Bedroom. Kitchen. Living room.

Before I have a chance to consider what any of it means, there is a flash of movement behind me. I turn to see that one of the mirrored walls has disappeared, replaced by a sheet of transparent glass. On the other side is a well-groomed man. It takes me a couple of seconds to place him. His rags are gone, as are his dreadlocks. Instead, he is dressed in a sharply tailored suit, his hair slicked back, his face freshly shaved and glowing with a mineral-enriched moisturiser. And there, on his left cheek, running from his temple to his jaw, is a scar.

'How's it going, dude?' Xan asks, his voice coming to me in crisp surround sound.

I scan the ceiling, spotting the concealed speakers, before I turn back to him. He is smiling at me now, his capped teeth glinting in the artificial light. He seems a little sleepy, his eyes pink, as if he's slightly high, or just woken from a nap.

'You okay?' he asks. 'You look like you've seen a ghost.'

I try to speak, but my voice is little more than a dry wheeze, the first strangled gasps of a panic attack.

'Hey, take it easy,' Xan chuckles. 'You need to breathe. Come on. Get your head between those legs. Take some deep breaths. Oxygenate that beautiful brain of yours.'

At this point, I double over and heave. There's not much to bring up. The room spins a couple of times before settling. I wipe the bile from my mouth.

'Feel better?' Xan asks, still beaming behind the glass.

'What's going on?' I say, the words stinging my oesophagus.

Xan raises an eyebrow. 'Really? Don't tell me you haven't figured this out yet?'

With enormous effort, I stagger towards him and slap my hand on the glass, smearing it with vomit. 'What. The. Fuck. Is. Going. On?'

Xan doesn't flinch. 'If I seriously have to spell everything out for you I will. Though I would remind you that, once again, this was all covered in the initial briefing documents that were supplied to you.'

'Briefing documents?'

'Jesus, Dave. How many times do we have to go over this? The terms and conditions. Section nine-point-four clearly states that MindCast Limited has a legal obligation requiring us to prevent foreseeable harm coming to the participant – that's you – and that, should it be deemed necessary, the Company will undertake decisive action in order to ensure they fulfil their obligated Duty of Care. In other words, we deemed it necessary to intervene in order to keep you safe. And not just so we can stay on the right side of the law, either. We care about you, Dave. Your wellbeing is our primary concern.'

'Keep me safe?' I groan, clutching my head. 'What did you do to me, Xan? What are you trying to keep me safe from?'

Xan chuckles. 'From yourself, silly. I mean, trying to pay someone to kidnap you? You were quite clearly delusional. Where the hell did you think you were going to go, dude? Back to the wilderness to get in touch with your primal self? To live off the land like some nouveau-caveman? Don't forget, I've seen your videos. You couldn't hunt and gather a Pot Noodle.'

I think back to the hut, to the pigeon I caught, cut and cooked myself. The sense of satisfaction I'd felt. Reflected in the glass, I can make out the outline of the gas stove and sleeping bag.

'So what are you saying? That the last few weeks... weren't real?'

'Hey bro. Come on. Just because something didn't actually *happen* doesn't make it any less real. That hunger? That thirst? Your pain and suffering? All of those emotions were totally valid in so much as you experienced them. They were real to you. As were the lessons you learned along the way. Resourcefulness. Emotional resilience. Those are yours to keep. No one can take those away from you, Dave. You've grown as a person. I'm actually proud of you...'

'Enough of the bullshit, Xan. I just want to know the truth for once. Was the whole thing just made up? What was it? Virtual reality?'

Xan grimaces. 'You know I've always despised that term. It suggests an inferiority of experience, don't you think? As if what we see around us now is any less virtual than what you just experienced. As if what we think of as consciousness is anything but our brain's pathetic attempt to shrink the world around us into something tangible. I mean, *good luck with that*, right? It's like asking a pocket calculator to display the contents of the Universe. No, I prefer the term 'alternative' reality. Or parallel simulation, maybe? Anyway, the point is that while Paul and I were developing the M900 chip, we discovered an interesting quirk. As well as being able to collect and transmit data about your thought patterns, it also works in reverse. Instead of just sending out data, it can receive data too. In effect, this means we can upload custom content to it so that it overrides your usual sense of perception.'

'Custom content? You mean you hacked my brain?'

'Amazing, right? I mean, it's early days yet. We've still got a few bugs to work through. The biggest issue we've found so far is rejection. If the content strays too far away from the subject's established sense of reality – breaking the laws of physics for example – the simulation has a tendency to break down. That's what you experienced back there, by the way. Things got too crazy so you "woke up". No, the best results we've achieved so far have come when we've stuck close to a subject's expectations of what they "should" be seeing. You wanted to go and live in the middle of nowhere, therefore we facilitated that for you. At least mentally. I mean, sure, physically you never actually...'

'I never actually left this room,' I say, finishing his sentence. To my surprise, I find I've begun to cry, hot tears streaking my cheeks.

'Hey, take it easy bro. I know you're a little frazzled, but you need to try and keep a perspective on things. You're a pioneer, remember? You don't think Chrissy Columbus had rough days? When he thought that he might have got it wrong and that his ship might just sail right off the edge of the world? You don't think Neil and Buzz might have had second thoughts once they were strapped into that rocket and they started counting back from ten? This is important work we're doing, the two of us.'

'The two of us? This had nothing to do with me. I was an unwilling participant in your stupid game.' I swallow a sob. 'You let me think that I got away. That I was free. When the whole time I was stuck here with you watching me, like some caged laboratory bunny. You... you lied to me.'

'Okay, first off let me just say that I acknowledge your emotions. Having said that, I'm afraid I have to refute the fact that anyone lied to you. Phase Two of the experiment was clearly flagged in the briefing documents, which again were checked and signed by yourself. This was always part of the agreed schedule. Your little "episode" just meant we brought it forward slightly. For your own safety. A less progressive organisation might have seen fit to have you sectioned or locked away in rehab once you started displaying such overt signs of psychosis. Instead, we provided you with a safe, immersive fantasy space where you could work through your problems, giving you a real shot at recovery. If anything, you should be thanking me.'

'Thanking you? I nearly starved to death. What happened to your concern for my wellbeing when you left me without food, huh?'

I'm shouting now, punctuating my argument by pounding on the reinforced glass that separates us. Xan only smiles though, seeming to grow calmer with each muted thump of my fist. He knows I can't go anywhere.

'I told you, I *was* concerned about your wellbeing. We all were. But there was only so much we could do about it. You see, at present the system only allows us to construct a simple scenario. We have limited input past that point. You're the one who forced it to play out as it did. We gave you free will, dude. Just like The Big Man. If you'd wanted to, you could easily have stumbled on an all-you-can-eat restaurant out there on your lonely meadow. It was you who *chose* to be tied up and starve. And do you know why? I think that, on some level, you wanted to suffer. You fetishised physical hardship, as if it might redeem you somehow. As if a rumbling belly might somehow offset the metaphysical hollowness you feel inside. That tedious, self-indulgent angst you've been boring half the planet senseless with for over a month now. Well let me clear something up for you, Dave. The suffering you underwent in the simulation is *nothing* compared to the pain and misery you would have experienced had you actually succeeded in getting yourself kidnapped and making it out to the wilderness. The truth is, you've never known real hunger. Real thirst. If you had, you'd have been down on your knees in a matter of hours, begging for us to take you back under our wing. To make it all go away. No, all in all, I think you were pretty lucky that we got to you when we did. Like I said, a little gratitude might be in order. Starting with your friend. After all, if she hadn't called us, who knows what might have happened?'

'My friend?' I mumble, the room beginning to lurch violently away from me.

'Sure. In fact, why don't you thank her yourself?'

Before I can say anything else, the mirror to Xan's right blanches white, then clears, revealing a woman in a smart blazer. A glowing band around her wrist. A silver employee badge pinned to her lapel.

She waves awkwardly. 'Hey David.'

'Alice? What the hell are you doing here?'

Xan beams. 'Alice got in touch with us the moment you told her about your crazy plan. She was worried about you. And rightfully so. Seeing as she's one of the people who knows you best, we invited her in as an advisor while we initiated our rescue operation. We quickly recognised her potential, however, and she's since agreed to join us on a full-time basis, replacing poor Katya as Deputy Product Manager. It was actually Alice's idea to insert the woodpigeon. Which was a technical nightmare by the way,' he laughs again. 'Like I say, you've got a lot to thank her for. If it had been left up to me, you'd have carried on starving.'

Ignoring Xan, I turn my attention fully to Alice, my voice dropping to an urgent whisper. 'You told them? After everything we talked about? I told you what they were capable of.'

'This is exactly what I was talking about, David,' she says. 'You were paranoid and hysterical. You weren't making any sense. You're one of the most recognised people on Earth. Did you really think some man in a van was going to help you drop off the face of the planet?

Besides, like Xan said, even if you had managed to somehow pull it off, you'd have probably ended up dead. I wanted to save you.'

'Oh, so you were saving me? And what, you thought you might as well apply for a job while you were at it?'

'That's not fair,' she says, still not meeting my eye. 'Besides, Xan reached out to me months ago. Around the time you were first fitted with the chip, actually. I thought you knew this? I remember coming to see you right after I'd met him.'

I think back to Alice standing in the doorway of my old apartment. How out of place she'd looked in her black party dress. 'You'd been to meet Xan *then*?'

'Let me guess? You thought I was dressed up like that just for you?'

'No, I mean, I just...' I stutter. 'But didn't you say you weren't interested in the job? That the client was a total creep?'

Alice shrugs. 'Xan made me an offer I couldn't refuse. Not to mention an opportunity to funnel my skills into something that's actually worthwhile for a change. I want to make a difference, David. Not spend the rest of my life chasing narcissistic D-listers. No offence.'

I shake my head. 'But what about everything you said? You've hated MindCast since day one. And you despise social media. You don't even *like* computers for crying out loud. And what about your writing? Please don't tell me you're doing this just for the money?'

At this she does look up, her face twisted in a sharp scowl. 'I really don't think you're in a position to judge my financial choices.' She sighs, softening slightly. 'Look, I've been treading water for almost a decade now. Doing something I hate just to keep from going under. Meanwhile, my own writing's going nowhere. Even if I did have the energy to finish my novel, who would read it now? That world is dead and buried.'

I feel my eyes beginning to sting. 'But what about *our* book?' I ask in a small voice.

'I quit,' she shrugs. 'Xan helped me pay the advance back in full. Hey, don't look at me like that. I just couldn't do it. Even with access to your every thought, I couldn't make it work. I couldn't pull it together. I'm sorry.'

'But you said… you said you were almost finished?'

'I know. And I was. In fact, the book will still probably come out. I let my publisher hang on to my drafts and research. They'll probably just assign it to another writer. Maybe it'll even be a real writer this time, not some washed-up hack like me.' She smiles sadly. 'Hey, look on the bright side. At least this way you've got an ending now.'

'Oh great.' I stare around my mirrored cage in exaggerated disbelief. 'So *this* is how my story ends? With me as a prisoner? As a human experiment?'

'No, dude,' Xan cuts in. 'As a hero.'

I scan his face for signs of snigger, a punch line. His eyes are shining though.

'Are you fucking crazy?'

'I'm totally serious. Like I said before, we're doing important work here. I'm not just talking about therapeutic applications either, although as you've experienced first-hand, we're clearly going to revolutionise mental health care overnight. No, I'm talking about bona fide, Nobel Prize, world-shuddering shit, Dave. Pick any challenge facing humanity, anything at all, and there's an opportunity for this new technology to be part of the solution. Crime? Terrorism? We'll know what people are planning even before they do. Overpopulation? No problem. We could keep people living in wardrobes and they wouldn't care. They'll think they're in a palace. Starvation? We can transform a crust of bread into a three-course dinner. Water into wine. No one need ever be hungry again – or bored or lonely or isolated for that matter. We're talking about creating a limitless universe inside each and every person's head. A truly inclusive utopia for all. A virtual heaven, right here on Earth.'

'Oh right,' I sneer. 'So you're going to convince everyone on the planet to undergo brain surgery just so they can live in a virtual world? Good luck with that.'

'Are you kidding? We've had literally millions of people sign up for the second season of MindCast. Seems everyone's just dying to share their thoughts with the world. Everyone wants to be the next you, Dave.'

'Second season?'

'Why not? Only this time there won't just be one star of the show. There'll be hundreds. Thousands maybe. And after that, who knows? You were always just the pilot, bro. A showcase for what's possible. Or rather, what *was* possible. You see the M900 chip is already looking as clunky and outdated as the first model of the OptimiZer band. Call it Moore's law or whatever, but the breakthroughs are coming in days rather than years. Only this morning, Paul was telling me about his research into genetically modified brain parasites. Apparently he's been working with this really nasty variety of amoeba. Usually they live in warm rivers and springs, where they occasionally make their way up people's noses and proceed to eat their brains. Anyway, he seems to think that with only a tiny adaptation we'll be able to reprogram them to deliver a nano-sized version of the chip. Imagine that. Instead of invasive surgery, MindCast becomes as simple and harmless as a flu vaccination. A quick spray up the nose and that's it, boom, you're plugged in for life. Once the costs come down, and they will, there'll be nothing stopping us from implementing universal coverage within a generation. We could give it to children along with their MMR jab. The second a baby takes their first breath. Just think of the possibilities...'

I think back to the attack in my old apartment, something Edward Corvin said.

How long do you think it'll be before MindCast goes mass market? Before it's mandatory? Before we're implanting chips at birth?'

I once again picture a baby's head clamped in a surgical vice, a trail of wires snaking out from the back of its skull.

'The sheep was right.'

'Oh, please,' Xan snorts. 'That sheep was an Oxford-educated fraud rebelling against his rich daddy. He's about as Marxist as Ronald McDonald.'

'Sorry. I forgot you were such a philanthropist. So I suppose you won't be taking advantage of that "universal coverage" to sell universal advertising space?'

For the first time since I've been here, Xan's smile falters. 'Really? I show you the greatest evolutionary tool since the Internet and you're going to argue about how it's funded? Sure, we might choose to align ourselves with a couple of likeminded commercial partners to ensure we remain financially viable. But this has never been about adverts.'

'It's about saving the world,' Alice says, finishing his sentence. 'And you can be part of this incredible opportunity, David. Don't you see? This isn't a product. It's a movement. And you can be at the head of it. A global ambassador, spreading the word.'

Xan nods in agreement. 'You either ride the crest of the wave, or you drown in it. So what do you say, buddy? Are you with us?'

I look from him to Alice, a pair of pulpit preachers, each of them ablaze with the same breathless righteousness. 'Do I have a choice?'

Xan and Alice both turn to each other and laugh.

'There he is,' Xan says, the smile returned to his face. 'There's the guy we all fell in love with all those months ago. I knew you'd see sense, bro.'

He takes his phone out and stabs at the screen. Seconds later, the glass between us peels back.

Tentatively, still not quite believing I'm free, I begin to walk forward towards the doorway. As I draw closer, I can see that Xan and Alice are standing in a long glass hallway. With a jolt, I realise I must be back at MindCast's headquarters. I wonder if the van took me straight here. If there even was a van. At what point did it all stop being real?

'Man, we've got so much to talk about,' Xan is saying. 'But first, why don't you grab a few hours of shut eye? You've had a heck of a few days. We've already got a room made up for you in one of the offices back here. You could probably do with a shower and a change of clothes too. No offence.'

It's surprisingly dark in the hallway, and looking up I'm able to make out a dim sliver of moon through three or four floors of glass. It occurs to me I have no idea what time it is, let alone the day.

As I reach them, Alice rests a hand gently on my shoulder. 'You know what, I'm pretty much wiped out myself. I might have a lie down with you. If that's okay?' she smiles, a look in her eye I've never seen before. I watch in surprise as she slowly runs her tongue across her bottom lip.

'That's a great idea Ali,' Xan says. 'Although you two love birds better get some sleep too. After all, we've got a big day tomorrow. We're going to change the world.'

He turns to me, laughing, his hand reaching for my other shoulder. He squeezes it affectionately. 'Seriously though,

I'm glad to have you on board. You've totally made the right decision. You won't regret it.'

I nod.

'Oh, I know I won't.'

And with that, I shrug them both off me, take a step backwards, and punch Xan as hard as I can.

Alice screams, while Xan doubles in two, his face streaked with blood.

'Wait,' he splutters. 'Come back.'

But I've already started to run.

The corridors are a maze. Within seconds I'm lost and out of breath, gasping for air as I sprint onwards into the darkness, desperately searching for a way out. It's no good though. Every office I run through looks the same. Every set of stairs just like the one before. Not far behind me, I hear the slap of Italian leather on a glass floor, along with the occasional unintelligible shout.

Xan.

I keep running.

Up ahead I reach a set of double doors. I dive for the handle, but the door won't budge. I search desperately for something to open it with, but find only the tongue scanner. After prodding uselessly at the buttons for a moment, I abandon the doors altogether, heading back down the corridor and up another flight of stairs. Suddenly there's an explosion of sound, a deafening high-pitched wail that cuts through the air, forcing my hands to cover my ears. An alarm. Seconds later, the corridors are lit up by a dim red light that strobes on and off in time with the siren, transforming the staircase into a stuttering zoetrope. Xan sounds closer now, his footsteps joined by others. I hear the static crackle of security guards' radios. The bark and snap of Dobermans' jaws.

I keep running.

At the top of the stairs I find myself in another corridor. I barrel forwards, not stopping to check where I'm going. I can no longer see the moon above me. I can't make out the sky at all, the security lights blinding me to everything but my next step forwards. I take another set of stairs, then another, but they are all heading in the wrong direction:

Up

Up

Up

I am travelling higher and higher inside the building, further and further from the exit, from freedom. But still the alarm rings out. Still the red light strobes. Still the footsteps pound, the radios buzz, the dogs bark. I pass through more corridors, more offices, more stairs, my chest burning, my legs cramping. I feel like I'm going to vomit again, or pass out, or both. I do neither though, fear motivating me to keep running keep running keep running keep running...

At the end of a long corridor, I reach another set of double doors. I fumble for the handle, more in hope than anything else. To my surprise, this time the door swings back. Without hesitation I dive through. And then I freeze.

On the other side of the door, I find myself standing at yet another identical corridor. Glass ceiling, walls, floor. Though it is difficult to make much out with the red light flashing overhead, it looks like it leads on to another set of featureless offices, and beyond that another set of stairs. It is not the offices or the stairs that have brought me staggering to a stop, though. Rather, it is the open doorway that lies a little further up the corridor, something disturbingly familiar about the sterile white light that is spilling out of it. Though I don't want to look, I find myself edging forwards. As I draw level with the doorway, I take a deep breath and poke my head inside.

Even though I already know what I'll find, it's still a shock to see the mirrored room again. My sleeping bag still rolled out in the corner. The camping stove still surrounded by empty wrappers. As impossible as it seems, I have come full circle. I have run all the way back to where I started.

It's then that I hear it.

Underneath the other sounds, the alarm, the footsteps, the radios, the dogs, there is something else. Something low and metallic, like the crunch and grind of distant cogs and gears.

Backing away from the mirrored cage, I hurry down the corridor and into the nearest office. Sliding behind a standing desk, I push my face to the far wall, cupping my hands to my eyes. It's difficult to make out anything at first. The office seems to be positioned deep within the orb, surrounded by a dozen or so other rooms. From where I'm standing it's impossible to make out either the sky or the courtyard below. I keep staring out, even as the approaching footsteps grow louder, closer, until finally, I spot a flicker of movement high above me. Suddenly there's another movement, closer this time. I watch with a mixture of horror and amazement as a staircase a few rows over begins to shift, dropping down a floor so that it leads to another doorway. Meanwhile, the office it had originally been connected to also begins to move, rotating until it joins onto another corridor, which in turn has latched onto a different set of stairs. The whole building is alive, I realise. Turning. Twisting. Reshuffling itself constantly, like a glass Rubik's Cube. Tricking me. Trapping me.

I turn to leave, only to see that the doorway I entered through is no longer there.

With a jolt, I realise the office I'm standing in has changed position too, turning so slowly that I didn't notice it moving. The security guards are so close now that I can make out odd words and phrases crackling from their radios, Xan's voice echoing and distorted:

… Capture… Third floor… Alive…

I begin to panic, my hands sliding over the smooth surface where minutes earlier there had been a door. I scan the room, looking for another way out. There's nothing though. I'm sealed in.

Dogs snarl.

Boots stomp.

Gears grind.

This is it, I think to myself. This is where it ends. In a soulless, minimalist workspace surrounded by orthopedically optimised chairs and neon coloured exercise balls. Then I have an idea. In the middle of the room is a low coffee table, a slab of glass mounted on a steel tripod. I take hold of it by one leg. With an immense effort, I drag it across the room, before hoisting it up into the air. I pause for a second. And then I launch it at the glass wall.

The table bounces straight back off, forcing me to dive out of the way. To my despair the glass remains intact. There's not even a scratch. I lift the table, and again hurl it with all my might. This time it connects well. There is a satisfying crack as it strikes the glass, the pane instantly fracturing into tiny cubes, like a disintegrating iceberg. I swing my leg out, aiming a single kick at the pane, and the entire wall explodes into a million granular pieces, leaving nothing but an empty frame. Stepping over the carnage, I dash through to the next office, which is identical in layout to the one I've just left. Again, I heave the coffee table from the floor. This time the wall gives at the first attempt. I step through to the next office and repeat the procedure again and again. Even with the rooms pivoting and rearranging themselves around me, they can't stop me. I fling myself onwards, bursting through each room in a blur of sweat and broken glass.

At last I reach an office that feels different. Even with the red light flashing above, I can see I have come to an edge. To the end. I press myself to the glass. Far below I am able to make out a dozen or so torchlights sweeping the darkness.

Security guards.

Behind me, the footsteps are so loud they almost drown out the alarm.

They're almost here.

I step back from the window and scan the room. This time there is no coffee table. Searching around for something I can use instead, I manage to wrench loose a water cooler from its base, using the last of my fading strength to charge at the far wall. On the third strike, the glass shatters, sending a shower of crystal cubes dazzling through the night air, onto the courtyard below.

I stick my head through the empty frame, surprised at the height of the drop beneath me. I must be twenty floors up. Down in the courtyard, the torchlights have converged into a single point, all aiming up at me. I ignore them, leaning further out of the building. The air outside is noticeably cooler, though beads of sweat continue to drip from my hair and into my eyes. Wiping my face, I reach out a hand, trying to feel for something to grip on to. It's no good though. The walls of the building are completely smooth.

The security guards are almost here now, the dogs and the boots and the radios just behind me. I can hear them just beyond the door. I only have minutes left.

Seconds.

Peering up, I spot a thick steel cable high above my head. I stretch up onto tiptoes, but it's too high to reach. I put one foot onto the frame of the window. And then I stop. I'm too late.

They're here.

Very slowly, I turn around to face the door.

There is no army of security guards, though. No snarling dogs or crackling radios. It's just Xan.

'Come on, David,' he says. 'It's time to go.'

I turn my back on him.

And then, without a word, I jump.

Though the orb is still flashing a furious red, I can no longer hear the alarm. I can't hear anything. In fact, it is curiously silent up here. A light breeze is blowing, and my shirt flaps open, sending a chill through my bones. Worried that a strong gust will be enough to dislodge me, I tighten my grip around the cable, using my momentum to swing my legs up and coil myself around it, so that my head is hanging upside down. Down in the courtyard the torchlights have scattered apart, the guards below seeming to dash in skittering circles, like startled fireflies.

I look away. Beyond them, there is something else; a giant screen standing roughly opposite the entrance. Tilting my head, I am able to make out a familiar silver logo in the corner of the display. Above it, there is a picture of me dangling from the glass orb. The image zooms in to show my blanched knuckles, as one by one my fingers peel loose and then I plunge in slow motion, pirouetting silently through the darkness. I see my body, broken and bleeding on the cracked cobblestones, then stiff and pale, wedged awkwardly into a coffin. I see my mother's face, her mascara running down her cheeks. I see my father's disappointment. Nadeem's indifference. I see the world disappear as I'm lowered into the ground and covered in a blanket of soil. I see myself on the cover of a thousand newspapers and magazines.

While all of this is playing out – my deepest fears, my darkest premonitions – the counter in the corner of the screen continues to rattle ever higher. More than a billion people are watching. In spite of everything, I can't help but feel a swell of pride. They're my highest ratings yet.

'David!'

Below me, Xan's face appears in the shattered window. Although his eyes are swollen black and his nose is crusted with dried blood, he's smiling. 'Come on, dude,' he calls out to me. 'There's nowhere to go. It's over.'

I shake my head, hugging the steel cord even tighter. 'Go away,' I shout back.

'This is insane, Dave. Just come inside and we'll work this whole thing out.'

'Oh, sure. And you and your hired thugs will just let me waltz right out the front door.'

His smile vanishes, replaced by a dark scowl. 'And why should I let you go? After you've attacked me and smashed up my building. You Brits have got a hell of a way of showing your gratitude, I'll give you that.'

'Gratitude? And what is it exactly I'm supposed to be grateful for?'

'Oh I don't know? For making you more famous than you could ever imagine? For making you wealthy beyond your most debauched fantasies?'

'For butchering Katya when she tried to warn me the chip was dangerous? For murdering Sarah when she was only trying to help me?'

Xan laughs sourly. 'Jesus, will you listen to yourself? You're sick, David. Sick and paranoid. You need to come down from there before someone gets hurt.'

'You killed my friends.'

'I didn't kill anyone. Now I know you want to believe this is all some Machiavellian conspiracy, but it's simply not true. All I care about is making the world a better place.'

'No matter who stands in the way?'

'No. Listen, Sarah was a great manager with an unfortunate predilection for prescription opiates. It was never going to end well for her. Katya on the other hand was a much-loved employee who was sadly attacked by a deranged member of the public. A fanatic. A digital luddite, lashing out at a world they don't understand anymore. That's leaving them behind. Just like that fraud Ed Corvin, they thought that by assaulting poor Katya, they could make a difference. They could halt progress. But you can't stand against the tide, Dave...'

Xan keeps talking, but I have stopped listening. I look down, searching the courtyard for the giant display. On the screen, I see I'm no longer dying. No longer falling or being buried. Instead, I am stepping back through the window. I am shaking Xan's hand and returning to my old life, only bigger, richer, more famous than ever before. I see a second season of MindCast playing out, then a third, a fourth. I see hundreds of new contestants, thousands, all of them streaming their thoughts day and night, with new volunteers signing up by the hour, the second. I see me as a pundit, a talking head chattering over choice highlights, offering unique insight and guidance on how to succeed on the biggest show on Earth. The only show on Earth.

I see an endless stream of adverts.

I see a generation held ransom by their thoughts. Edited. Censored.

I see reality smothered, a fake world grafted on top of our own.

Xan continues to rattle on. He is talking about IPOs and market capitalisation. He is talking about new territories and opportunities for expansion.

He is talking about the future.

Without saying anything, I uncurl my legs from around the cable and let myself drop, so that I am hanging above the courtyard by only my hands.

Xan trails off, the colour draining from his face.

'You know that's really fucking immature, Dave.'

I don't say anything.

'So what? You're going to kill yourself now? Well be my guest. I mean it. The final thoughts of a dying man streamed live around the world? It'll be a televisual sensation. This is the moon landing times a hundred. Diana's funeral times a thousand. The ratings will be through the roof.'

Still I ignore him. My hands are aching now. My fingers cramping. The steel fibres digging into my palms. I close my eyes and focus on the gentle breeze that is playing through my hair, cool and sweet.

'For God's sake come inside,' Xan yells, all pretence of calm detachment disappearing. 'You're being ridiculous. Doing this won't make the blindest bit of difference. The technology inside you is already obsolete. We don't need it anymore. This thing is going to happen, whether you choose to be part of it or not. We are going to change the world, David.'

At last I turn my head, open my eyes, meet his gaze. Standing in the hollowed window frame, he looks smaller and shabbier than I remember, his tie hanging loose around his neck, his tailored shirt splattered with blood. His bruised face is screwed up tight with rage, but there's no anger in his eyes. There is only fear.

'Choose?' I laugh. 'That's the whole point, Xan. I don't have a choice. Not really. I never have.'

I open one hand. Instantly, my body swings to one side, sending a sharp jolt of pain through my shoulder and bicep.

'No! Dave, wait. You're making a terrible mistake...'

My whole body is shaking now, my muscles screaming with the effort of hanging on. With the last of my strength, I lift my head and look Xan in his swollen, scared eyes. 'You're probably right,' I say, my words flecked with spit, spoken through gritted teeth. 'But at least it's my mistake to make.'

I let go.

⁂

I fall for the longest time.

As I tumble through the darkness, I catch a glimpse of the screen below.

I don't know what I'd expected to see. Memories? Regrets? A life lived in reverse?

There is none of that.

There is only a single, perfect cloud, getting bigger and bigger as I rush towards the ground, while in the bottom corner, the view counter scrolls faster and faster until it becomes a red blur, two billion, three billion, the whole world watching.

And still the cloud grows bigger, spilling from the screen and then bursting free from it, filling the courtyard, engulfing the building, the entire city, until there's nothing else. Nothing else.

Turning the night to day.

The darkness to light.

Until there is nothing but beautiful, brilliant, boundless…

White.

PART SIX

Blink.

I'm awake.

Not only that...

I'm alive.

I sit up. Cough. Choke. Look around.

In the far corner of the mirrored room is my sleeping bag. Still rolled out. Still looking recently slept in. Nearby is still my rucksack, spare clothes still spilling from the top. Still the camping stove, the frying pan, the empty food packets.

And there, still standing at the window, peering in at me, are Xan and Alice.

'Hey dude. So now that you've got *that* out of your system, you'll understand why we couldn't possibly risk letting you go. You're just too unstable. Too unpredictable.'

I'm up and over at the window in four steps. Beating at

the glass. Yelling. Screaming. 'You lied to me. You fucking lied to me again. You let me think I was free…'

Xan chuckles as I continue to thump the glass. His nose is no longer broken. His shirt is no longer speckled with blood.

'That's debatable. Like I said, we're only capable of providing the most basic of scenarios at the moment. Everything else was you. If anything, you lied to yourself.'

This time I punch the glass so hard I feel something give. My knuckle cracking, caving in on itself. I let out a yelp. Double over in pain.

'For crying out loud,' Alice chides. 'There's no point hurting yourself. It won't change anything.'

I look up at her, squinting through my tears. 'How could you?' I sob. 'How could you let him do this to me?'

She raises a stern eyebrow. The softness has gone from her face now. She is cold. Uncaring. 'Oh, do give it a rest. You've only got yourself to blame. Perhaps if you weren't so terminally selfish things might have worked out differently.'

'Selfish?'

'You had a chance to speak to the whole world, David. You could have used that position to achieve anything you wanted. You could have used your influence to bring the world together. To champion the weak and downtrodden. You could even have brought down MindCast if you really wanted to. But you didn't, did you? No, you were content to fill your head up with nothing but white noise. Inane,

meaningless fluff. With the bar set so low, it's hardly surprising that in the end nobody even noticed you'd gone.'

'I don't understand?' I sniff.

'You mean to say you haven't wondered why there hasn't
been a global outcry? Why nobody noticed when you went
wandering in the virtual wilderness for a week? Why your
adoring public haven't scaled the building and demanded
we set you free?'

I blink once, twice. 'I... I...'

'Okay, dude,' Xan says, holding up his hands. 'You got
us. The truth is we switched the feed. All people have been
watching for the last few weeks is... Well here, see for
yourself.'

He stabs at his phone. Instantly an image appears
on the far wall. It's me reaching for a beer. An ice-cold
Budweiser. The bottle clammy with condensation. A hint
of foam around the tip.

'Adverts?' I croak.

'Twenty-four hours a day,' Xan grins. 'After your disap-
pearance, we had to fill the airtime in a hurry. We didn't
have time to plan anything more sophisticated. So we put
the commercials on loop and waited for the backlash from
the public. But here's the crazy thing. Your viewing figures
actually improved. More people are watching your show
than ever. Not that it's really your show.'

'What do you mean?' I snap. 'Of course it's my show. It's
my brain that people tune in to every day. It's my thoughts
that have made MindCast a success.'

Xan shrugs. 'Maybe. Although, if you're brutally honest with yourself, I think you know that we could have plugged pretty much anyone into that chip and the show would still have been a hit. Actually, we almost did.'

'Did what?'

'Come off it, bro. You didn't really think you were our first choice, did you? This thing took years to develop. It cost hundreds of millions of dollars. You think we did all that hard work just so we could take a peek into your specific, not-terribly-exciting brain? I mean, sure you ticked a lot of boxes. You were based in the UK for one thing. There's far less pesky legislation and regulations to get around here than over in the States. And having your own ready-made fan base was certainly a bonus. Then there were your commercial interests, which overlapped neatly with our own aspirations. At least at first. But then, so did lots of people's. In fact, we had a shortlist of dozens before we settled on you. Hundreds. We just worked our way down. All the movie stars refused, of course. Too much to lose. Too many skeletons in their closets. No rapper or rock star would touch it either. We even asked that friend of yours. What's his name again? Nadeem?'

'You spoke to Nadeem?' I croak.

'Sure. He's young. Handsome. Scored highly with our test audience. We thought he'd be a great fit. So we invited him out here. Gave him the whole pitch. He turned us down though. He wasn't convinced. Thought this was just some novelty that would interfere with his culinary career. I'd imagine he was insanely jealous once he saw you blow up.

Thinking about it, that's probably why he ended up falling out with you...'

'He never said a word about it.'

Xan smiles. 'And that's precisely what we pay the lawyers so much for. Anyway, the point is you were the first one who actually said yes. The only one, in fact. Believe it or not, most people seemed to think this was all a pretty bad idea.'

Xan pauses. Grins.

'So you see, this has never really been about you at all, dude. You've always been... interchangeable.'

I stare at him, open mouthed. 'So what now?' I ask at last.

Xan's smile fades. 'Ah. Well that's where things get a little complicated. I mean obviously, we can't let you go. At least not yet.'

'What do you mean? You can't just keep me here indefinitely.'

'Why not? It's not like anyone's going to notice.' Xan points to the screen. Already the beer commercial has been replaced by a picture of me wearing a pair of state-of-the-art noise cancelling headphones, my head tilted back, my eyes closed in bliss.

I turn to Alice. 'You've got to stop this. You can't let him do this to me.'

'Sorry David,' she says. 'But I'm afraid he does have a point. We're working to build a better planet here. It seems you're simply not mature enough to understand that.'

She gives a final, sad smile and then disappears, the glass window becoming a mirror behind her.

I turn back to Xan. 'So that's it? You're just going to abandon me here? In this… this cage?'

'Well, I guess that's up to you, dude. I could send you back to your hut if you like? Hell, I could send you to a tropical paradise if it made you happy? That's the beauty of this thing, Dave. *Here* doesn't have to mean *here* anymore. It's only a cage because you're choosing to see it that way.'

I shake my head furiously. 'So what? I'm supposed to go and live in some fake bubble? Some fantasy world?'

Xan shrugs. 'Whatever, dude. If you feel so strongly about it, you can just stay here.'

He turns to leave, then pauses.

'Oh hey, I wanted to ask you something. How do you know any of *this* is real?'

I blink. 'What do you mean?'

Xan spreads his hands, gesturing towards the room. 'This place. This *cage,* as you so dramatically call it. Hell, this whole conversation. I could have programmed it all. It could just be taking place in your head and you'd never know, right?'

I don't say anything. I just stare.

He smiles.

'Anyway, it's just something to think about. Seeing as you're going to have so much time on your hands now,' he turns to leave again. 'I'll guess I'll be seeing you around, bro.'

And with that, he is gone.

'Wait!' I scream. 'Wait!'

I rush to the window, running my hands over the glass, clawing at it. Searching for cracks. For gaps. For any way out. It's hopeless though. There is nothing but my face, reflected in every surface, repeated over and over again.

Hours pass. Years.

I keep looking.

Clawing.

Searching.

But there is only ever me, me, me.

ACKNOWLEDGEMENTS

This book was written quickly, in a state of heightened anxiety. Huge thanks, and occasionally huge apologies, are due to the following:

My family, friends and siblings.

My parents, for their love, guidance and endless encouragement.

Lauren Smith for her helpful comments on early drafts. Dr Chris Jones for his psychological/neurological insights. Chris Oakley at Netitude for his technical input.

Fellow writers, for their support and inspiration along the way: Adelle Stripe, Ben Myers, Sam Mills, Michael Langan, Jim Crace, Stephen May, Kerry Hadley-Pryce.

Also: Jonathan Davidson at Writing West Midlands and all at Room 204, Aki Schilz and all at TLC, *LossLit*

Magazine, *Grist Anthology*, University of Greenwich, Oxford Brookes University, Absent Fathers and everyone else I've forgotten.

Everyone who still buys physical books.

Extra special thanks to Tom, Lauren, Lucy and all at Legend Press.

Finally, thanks to Simone. For everything.

Liam Brown's debut novel *Real Monsters* was published in 2015 and long-listed for the *Guardian*'s Not the Booker prize, followed closely by *Wild Life* in 2016.

He lives in Birmingham with his wife and two children.

Visit Liam at
liambrownwriter.com
Or on Facebook, Twitter or Instagram
@liambrownwriter